I0619701

The Independent Bookworm

ABOUT THE BOOK

In 2002 ADR, the jewel of the southern empire is Cryssigens where life is a constant carnival of display, while beneath the surface brews a world of intrigue and rebellion. Nobles, guilds and the House Cups scheme with and against each other even in the best of times. Since the recent civil war, the city and kingdom are stripped of their Overlord, and the parties dare all in a bid to succeed to the throne.

When the elven lords, preachers and merchants of Cryssigens need wrongs righted without clues, they look for the stealthic Feldspar to solve their problems. But the legend without a face is hard to find: and when Feldspar takes a commission from the most famous and beautiful priestess in the city, he finds problems of his own piling up. Feldspar's exploits not only take him to the ancient city below, he also must reinvent himself and is forced to choose between Hope and safety.

"Fencing Reputation" is the second story in the Shards of Light saga set in the Lands of Hope.

ABOUT THE AUTHOR

Will Hahn has been in love with heroic tales since age four, when his father read him the Lays of Ancient Rome and the Tales of King Arthur. He taught Ancient-Medieval History for years, but the line between this world and others has always been thin. The far reaches of fantasy, like the distant past, still bring him face to face with people like us, who have choices to make.

Will has written about the Lands of Hope since his college days (which by now are also part of ancient history). He chronicled the adventures of Solmn Judgement dilligently in two tomes of over 1000 pages each (it's now being published as an eBook series and in print) and his Shards of Light series, a sword and sorcery story. He also chronicled stand alone stories like "The Plane of Dreams" or "Three Minutes to Midnight." More of Will's tales of Hope are available at several online retailers.

Find out more on his website: www.WilliamLHahn.com

FENCING REPUTATION
Shards of Light
Volume II

William L. Hahn

Fencing Reputation, Shards of Light II
– second edition –
published by the Independent Bookworm, USA und D
this book is also available as eBook at various retailers

printed On-Demand Publishing LLC, 100 Enterprise Way, Suite A200,
Scotts Valley, CA 95066, USA, www.createspace.com

ISBN-13 978-3-95681-095-4

Find more information on the publisher's website:
http://www.IndependentBookworm.de

To Mitch Katz, a hero who knows a thing or three about taking on a new life, thinking quickly, dealing with money, and Risk in the service of Hope.

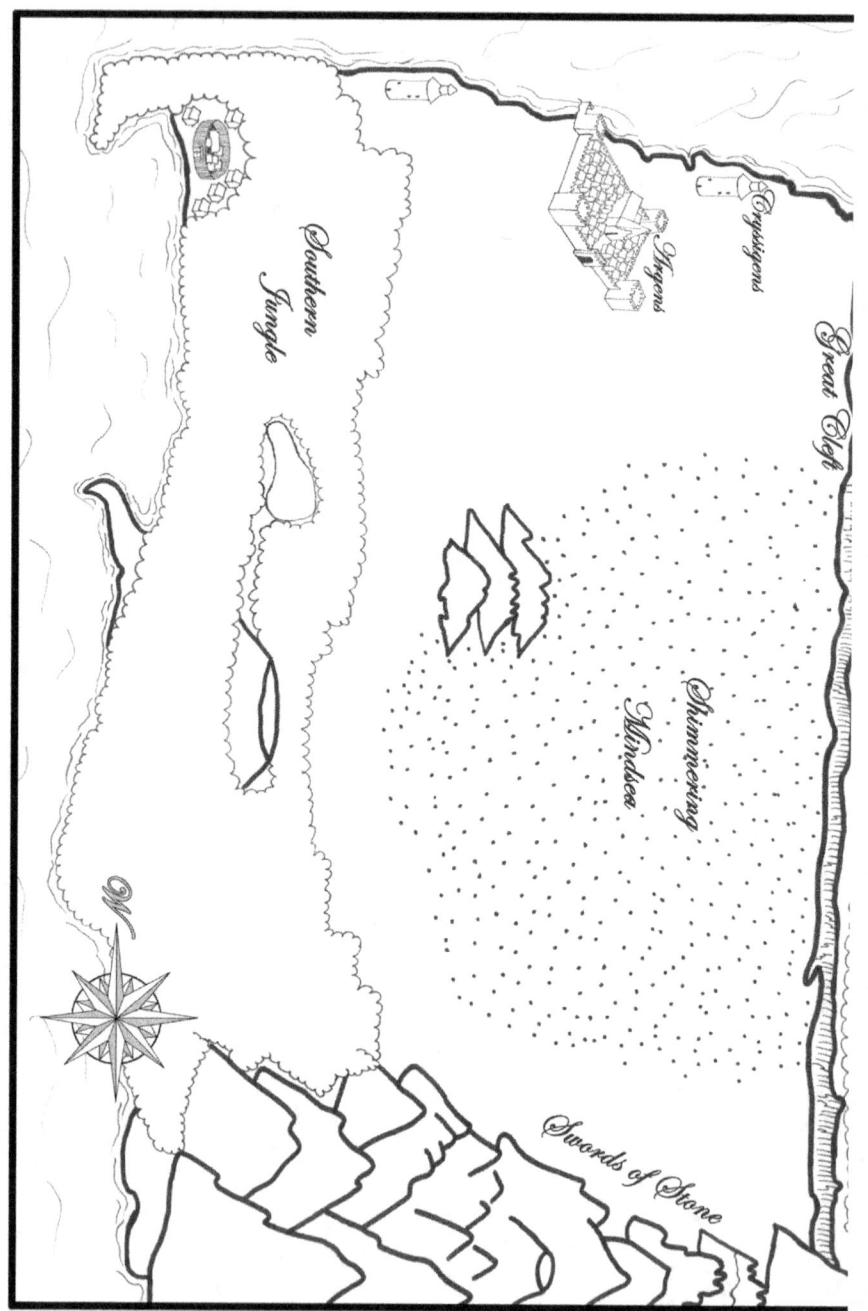

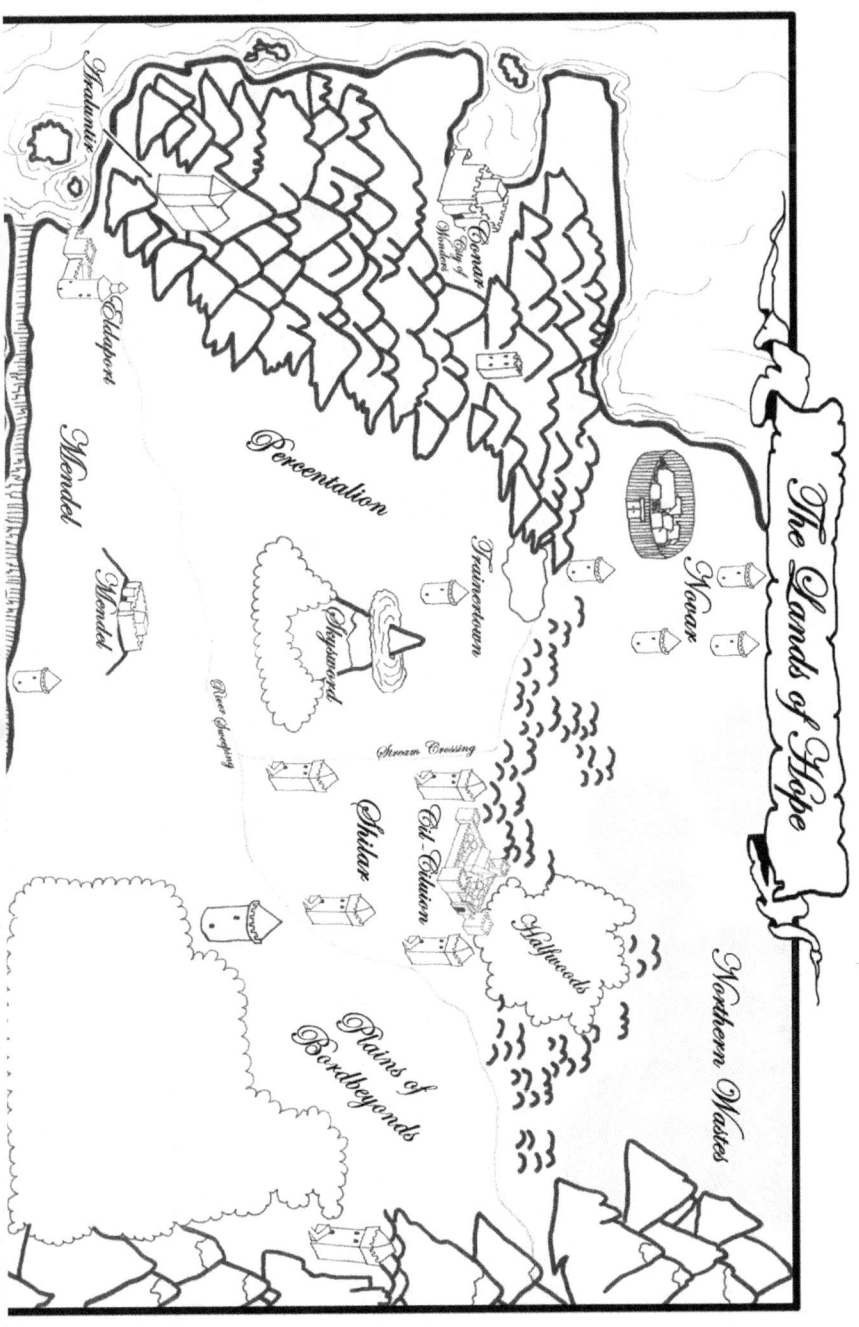

The Lands of Hope

CAST OF CHARACTERS IN ORDER OF APPEARANCE

Stealthic Feldspar	elf, disguised professional known across Cryssigens but never seen
Dekentar Beirill	elf, city guardsman, sworn to capture Feldspar
Jonn Simith	stone merchant, meek, plain-faced elf recently moved to The Boards
Noudhal	elf, innkeeper of The Grog's Lees
Keilee Staveshaver	elf, youngest child of a barrelmaker
Talishaya Staveshaver	"Lashi", elf, eldest child of a barrelmaker and acolyte of the Stargazer temple
Droke Staveshaver	elf, barrelmaker of The Boards, Red House man
Giurid	elf, bricklayer of The Boards, Blue House man
Overlord Toll'k'r	elf, North Mark's ruler of centuries ago
Minstrel Tambouri Shai	elf, beautiful singer in Cryssigens
Smith Delith	elf, female smith and tavern regular
Emperor Yula	dwarf, also called the First or Usurper, ruler of the Argensian Empire
Stealthic Trekelny	human, greatest Stealthic of living memory, robbed Khoirah's temple and escaped the City of Heroes (*see Three Minutes to Midnight*)
W'starrah Altieri	elf, also called Heaven's Eye, Myster, High Priestess, "Star", and Lavender Lady, prophetess and famed beauty of Cryssigens, Purple House leader
Farlo	elf, street thug
Barkarr	elf, street thug, former gladiator
scribe Thalek Poronar	elf, procures Simith's new home
Patriarch Z'kammet Hammer	elf, leader of the church of Argens Hopeforger in Cryssigens
Cup Carnad Mias	elf, head of Red House in Cryssigens

Fire Grip Gaspar Heugen	elf, virtual regent and leading member of the Blue House in Cryssigens
Chaktha	human, W'starrah's Nubian bodyguard
Curate Ekaterinye	"Kat", elf, Stargazer preacher, schoolteacher, and W'starrah's friend
Emperor Viridian XXVII	former emperor of Argens, demon in disguise, now slain
Overlord D'stagnon Kreel	elf, former Mark of the North, slain by Yula in 2001 ADR
Overlord Kreelon Kreel	elf, son of Kreel, died soon after
Myster Tarsi	elf, former leader of the cult of Argens Demonbender, slain in the rebellion
Highforge Mart'l'n Ecclese	elf, leader of Argensian worship of centuries ago, creator of the Brow of the Ecclesiast
Curate Knarg Spineslammer	elf, legendary preacher who failed the Brow test
Curate Tel Amaren	elf, Telholian preacher who became Highforge
Curate Kama	human, Telholian preacher building a chapel in Cryssigens, former member of the Candidates
Rainor	elf, High Alchemist of the empire, former Candidate
Imperial Mage Balen'th	Elf, feuding with F'liths
Imperial Mage F'liths	elf, feuding with Balen'th
Salivaar	leader of the bandit gang in Old Cryss

FENCING REPUTATION

*"No man can wear one face to himself and another to the multitude,
without finally getting bewildered as to which may be true."*
Nathaniel Hawthorne

Only my first day to try existing, and already it wasn't going well.

My face constantly prickled, out in full view. I kept putting my hand up to adjust a slipped eyebrow, or a chin-piece peeling loose, it was automatic. Air on my face, on all parts of my face? That meant something had gone wrong with my disguise. Only now I was the disguise—the face no one in Cryssigens had ever seen was on display. Feldspar the infamous stealthic, just sauntering down The Boards in the city's poorer quarter, taking in the air and daring any soul here to recognize me.

But what else could I do? Being a ghost just hadn't worked out.

I came to the end of Altair Way, the main thoroughfare of the dazzling, urbane new city and up till now the precinct of my former life. Here the cobbled boulevard emptied into The Boards, a street literally made of wood; I turned right along the wide planks bordering

11

the river to my left. Within twenty steps the crowd around me changed its character along with the altered sound of boots on wood, as I plunged among the lower classes.

I felt my neck muscles loosen bit by bit, and wondered why people here were not staring at me. In the center of Cryssigens, the idle wealthy and their plotting followers scrutinized everything that moved. In the center mall, how much red, how many in blue? That one there, the tall one, he's new; more soldiers than usual, I wonder what will happen. I did it all the time myself. My world, the one I had known for years was at my back. Everyone knew me there, though no one had ever seen me. I worked in the newer city, and would return to it soon, but only in one of my many disguises. That's where I'm needed; I'm a stealthic.

But folks here—that hopping fellow rolling the barrel over his own foot, the inn-keep adjusting his sign again as the children run laughing, the maiden looking for her sister. A trio of curses, one of them new to my ear. Everyone is… busy. With work! They labor! No time to plot, even less to suspect. As I reflected while strolling, I realized they did indeed look at me, all the time. But I simply met their gaze, we both nodded, and there an end. No one was looking *for* me.

And if a stranger merited a moment's glance, I had taken pains to be sure it was only one moment. My greatest weapon in avoiding discovery, without doubt, was my face itself. A nose not too straight, hair not very full, ears and eyes and mouth so plain and small and colorless—I had always been able to defy recollection. During my early days at the theater I found I could add any kind of prosthetic, new hair, pigments, wrinkles, and it all seemed natural because my face, by itself, was so lacking. My fellow actors called me The Mannequin, and addressed me while talking to their costume dummies in jest. Merely fifteen years later I had enough wealth to own the theater itself if I wanted: one of them passed by on the street last week and never recognized me. Of course, I was a woman at the time.

But clothing also made this man. A plain brown tunic, with dull green breeks, and covered sandals gave no clue to any House affiliation, any guild status, certainly showed no sign of wealth. And all my pockets are on the inside, easily reached behind the sash. Among these folk, who bent under loads, smelled of sweat, had a lot to do, and couldn't say what they were wearing without a glance down, I could relax. I had lost count of the turnings for my new house, but it didn't matter. I strolled along, taking note of landmarks, drinking in the view, feeling a touch of wonder at what it might mean, not to matter, not to hide.

I turned the corner and almost ran into the guardsman who had been seeking me for two weeks. Beirill, who worked for the Fire Grip, had been on duty when I slipped in and out of his master's house. Never mind I was invited. Guards like to think they do their jobs well, and this one had publicly sworn to bring me in.

With no time to react, I had to decide. Fight, out of the question— no merchant beats up a city guardsman with his bare hands. And flight, here in broad daylight, was a sure way to become news, and create dozens of suspicious people. Beirill loomed over me, shield on his back and spear leaning casually on a shoulder as he chatted with his partner. I had not wanted to test my new self so soon. This fellow had actually seen me—my form at a distance, anyway, outside the palace. There was nothing to do, except hope that nothing would be enough. I kept my pace and stride the same, held my course, met his gaze a moment, nodded at them both congenially.

Suddenly, nothing happened. The pair passed by, as if I were— nobody! The next instant, as my smile grew behind their backs, nothing continued to happen. The eatery near me had a few chairs and tables for patrons set outside. I had to sit, my legs felt a bit watery; I breathed deep and chuckled to myself, glancing only once or twice at Beirill's back. The man would have run a maze of knives to get half as close to the notorious Feldspar as he had come just now. Years of habit don't dissolve overnight—I still could not make my body understand that no cover was the best disguise.

The innkeeper came to ask me if I would eat, and I decided that I would. I asked breezily to see the bill of fare, and watched his thin face widen a bit with the effort of understanding me. Evidently most of his customers did not pose challenges.

"My bills, they're always fair."

"I mean, good sir, what have you to eat here?"

"My wife, she's made a fish stew today."

"Charming. And the choice?"

"Well," he said with some effort to be polite, "you can eat it. Or not."

"Very good!" I declared, "And do you have ale as well, by chance?"

I didn't expect him to catch my mood, but suddenly he got a grin on his face. "Truthfully no, sir; we have ale because I planned it that way." I laughed just a bit harder than I would have on my own, and waved my arm that he should bring it all. As the innkeep bustled off, I returned to watching the traffic of The Boards, my new neighbors. My heart was still beating quickly, as much from having such a normal conversation as meeting Beirill. The young lady was still seeking her sister, and I decided to spot the child if I could, though I had only a vague idea she would be younger and smaller. But the gaggle of kids playing a combination of tag, chase, and catch swirled about in plain sight, mostly boys; the rest were all adults as far as I could see.

"Your stew and ale, sir," said the innkeep and I extended my hand for him to clasp. "I am new to your precinct, my name is Simith." He quickly wiped his hands on his apron and returned my grip, which sent a click through me. I had heard about handshakes. "Noudhal, citizen Simith, and very pleased to meet you. Welcome to the Grog's Lees."

I took a gold piece from my inner pocket and snapped it down on the table; it had his undivided attention as I spoke. "I won't need change for this—in fact," I said trying my best to sound light and unconcerned, "I would rather set up a tab, if you follow me."

Noudhal wanted to follow me, I could tell, but was no better acquainted with modern finance than most of his fellow citizens. Still I was determined—carrying money was to be avoided at all costs, even the dozen or so coins I had with me today made me nervous. "Perhaps I can explain—won't you get an ale for yourself and sit with me?"

The thin man looked quickly around at his empty establishment and eagerly nodded. "I don't mind if I do, sir!" He ran off again, leaving the gold piece. Good. An honest man, at least.

"Keilee!" the young woman's yell was nothing new, she'd been calling for her sister constantly. But this one was aimed across the street in my direction, and I looked up. In one moment, I saw enough to raise Feldspar within me. Around the woman the wooden street, over her shoulder the outer railing of the Boards, and the dark fetid

14

river beyond and below. Abandoned dock pilings and shreds of the ruined bridge led the eye toward the abandoned old lower city. And atop a piling near that far side, behind the calling woman, a small figure teetered. Risk, in the service of Hope. Before I could think, the stealthic took over.

The entire scene blurred; in a moment I had crossed the crowded street, avoided a half-dozen people and stood on the rail over the river below. I was stuck; glancing back over my shoulder I could see the young woman—quite stunning, how could I not have noticed that—turning my way along with several others. They caught sight of the child now too, and their various useless shouts were spiced with more than normal concern. I had never before in my life looked on the old city across the river, but now I felt a twinge of something ancient and wrong. Everyone knew the stories.

"Can you help her, sir?" the young woman was frantic, and I cursed Feldspar's reflexes even as I dredged up Simith from wherever he'd been dunked. Trying to maintain a mask of inane geniality, I put myself back in the shoes of a normal everyday merchant of uninteresting stone, who somehow found himself in the ludicrous position of rescuing hero.

"Well, I hardly know, but will do my best, mistress," and with that I tried to look the fumblefoot as I leaped heavily but somewhat quickly from piling to piling along the path the child must have used. No good delaying—I needed to move fast to be of any use, and I could not do that while making myself seem inept. Stooping briefly I grabbed up a thin rod of driftwood leaning against a piling, and waved it about erratically as a balance-pole to explain my good fortune.

Clods of gulls hunching on any surface I wanted to use squawked at me and cleared away only at the last moment—I cursed their idiocy aloud and silently thanked them for adding to the chaos that could cover my actions. All the while the stealthic roiled inside me, chuckling at the minor difficulty of the acrobatics and cackling at the fraying of my scheme to conceal him from the world. Feldspar was famous, or rather infamous, and he wanted the credit no matter how it hashed my effort at disguise. In an instant I recalled the abandoned warehouse, and my attempt at the ghostly life, which came to such an abrupt halt just last week.

Life in the upper city had definitely been more comfortable. The warehouse stored my changing things, extra supplies, and some of my wealth. Plenty of room to practice acrobatics, or to measure out spaces for other feats I had in mind; praise Astor, the secret rooms were never discovered. If it hadn't been for my theatric habits, I might still be there. But scaring off the guards who came at night to drink and gamble seemed a good idea at the time.

Now I was in for it, one way or another. I stepped and half-leaped from stone pile to driven timber, holding a beat or two to make it seem difficult, and came closer to the little girl. She had finally realized the danger of her position, so close to the haunted ancient city and unable to make out the return path. She stood frozen, with no escape. I empathized with her plight, and just as I might have laughed at that irony, I slipped.

It happens to the best of us. Feldspar almost righted me before I could assert a clumsier self—waving the stick, I teetered and slowly fell with a helpless cry through a cloud of outraged gulls and into the dark, slow-moving stream. Under the water, I briefly reviewed my options.

The ability to swim is quite rare, and I certainly could not afford to add that level of attention to what I had already drawn. I had serious doubts that Simith would survive this day, no matter what—it might be best to let him drown. But through the murky water I could see the girl crouching down now on top of her piling, looking for me. Couldn't let her stay here, Feldspar forbade cowardice. No wonder I kept him for the night.

Wildly thrashing, I let the stick in my hand flail into view, and the girl did her part catching it as it swung by her piling. Careful not to tug on it with my full weight, I kicked under the surface and righted myself enough so that I could make a show of coming up, spitting water and clinging ridiculously to the timber she was on. Shouts and laughter from the Boards—another command performance.

I looked up at the child, perhaps eight by her face, a little scuffed and dressed poorly. What does a floundering, well-meaning stone merchant say to an adventurous scamp so close to the edge of nightmares? What would anyone say? I found I could barely speak to this urchin, certainly I could not lie. We were sharing risk, there were sacred obligations in play.

"I'm glad you caught the stick."

"You could get hurt doing that, mister." The girl seemed very serious, and I had to smile.

"You are absolutely right. But what are you doing here? Your sister has been looking for you."

The child shrugged, as if to say "that is why I'm over here", but said only "I'm Keilee".

I clawed my way to the top of the piling, and parked half my seat on it next to her. "Yes, I have heard your name today. I am—"

"You're the stone merchant," she interrupted, still so young for an elf and as hasty as a human. "You're moving in next door to us. You're citizen Simith," she said like an accusation. I smiled again and held out my hand.

"I hope you will call me Jonn." She solemnly took my hand and once again I felt a charge at the contact, and for telling the truth so far. Whatever else I showed the world, Jonn was indeed the name my parents had given me.

"Were you trying to reach the old city?"

She shook her head and hunched her shoulders as if to further block out the view. "Not at first, I was just exploring." I could see some real fear on her face now. She peered at me, a little suspicious. "Would you go there?"

I looked around behind us, and saw the old stone storage piers and the dry-dock lying empty as they had for centuries. Behind them further away from the river, buildings piled higher and thicker blocking the view of the grand municipal structures everyone said were at the interior. All deserted, plague-ridden, vermin-infested or haunted, depending on who you asked. Inside me the spirit of my evenings tingled with adventure. I still could not lie to that straight even face next to mine. "Well, that would be quite the expedition," I managed, gesturing weakly to one side, "that's pure porphyry there, unless I miss my guess, and for an outbuilding no less. I wonder why not limestone… though of course it would no longer stand if so." I let my knowledge of building stone take me safely into territory too boring for a child to follow. And she seemed suitably dulled by my speech, though I could see lights in her eyes still, not easily extinguished.

The crowd back on the Boards was discussing the matter in loud but indiscernible tones; some men had extended planks across to the first three pilings. Guards would drift by soon, and I did not want that. Gesturing to Keilee, I stood and took her on my back. She was alarmingly light; I have carried three treasures that weighed more. Still holding the useless stick, I made a show of measuring the distance, and carefully hopped from pile to pile. Gulls had of course reoccupied every perch I cleared on the way over, and were just as scandalized as before to move again. Behind us, the abandoned old city seemed to silently watch, and I felt a tingle in the base of my back that spoke of peril. Feldspar purred with delight, but I throttled him.

I gave the crowd a little show of losing my balance once; to my surprise the girl did not panic and kept her weight still, just as I would have asked. I heard her murmur in my ear, "That wasn't very hard."

I looked Keilee in the eyes as she loomed over my shoulder, and once again I could not keep truth from her. I nodded, saying "No, it seems we will make it after all." With this, she seemed oddly satisfied.

Keilee jumped down as soon as we reached the planks and jogged ahead of me to the railing. Her sister alternated hugging her head and slapping her wrist as I accepted some hands to negotiate the final barrier. My soaking-wet shoulders got thoroughly pounded by men who lifted heavy things for a living; I had planned to faint, but it wasn't going to be hard to fake with so little air in my lungs. The crowd cleared and Keilee's sister stood before me, one hand gripping the child's with white knuckles and her face simply beaming as she spoke words of gratitude in a fair, educated tone. I saw the symbol of the moon and star on her tunic, and realized she was an acolyte of the Stargazer temple. Her beauty began to make sense. Holding my breath to heighten the effect, I nodded, started to speak, then let my eyes roll up and fell straight to the Boards heedless of catching arms.

When people think you cannot hear they speak the truth of you.

"Astor's loins, what a fool, should have been killed."

"Is he alright? Keilee, get water from the Lees, hurry!"

"Who is this scatterhead anyway?" With a shock I recognized Beirill's deep voice.

"Haven't seen him—"

"He's the new fellow living on Byview, right behind my inn. Name's Simith."

"Never heard such a queer family. Be hard to forget that, even if he hadn't put on a show."

"He'll never forget today either, look at him, poor spineless little runt, he hasn't had such excitement in his life I'll bet."

"Citizen Simith? Can you hear me, are you alright?"

"Here's the water, can I go now?"

"You scamp, nearly the death of me, you won't leave my sight until I get you home to mother—"

"Lashi! I have to—"

"Not another word. And you will visit citizen Simith to offer your services at chores for a week."

"A week!"

"A month then, you demon minus a leg! Stay right here or I, I'll cook you."

The images I had in my mind of that fresh-faced child's outrage, or the radiant sister trying to twist her features into a fearsome scold, were too much. I had to laugh, but managed to turn it into a cough. As everyone turned back to me, I rolled to face down and went into the racking, meaty hack I used as the elderly beggar, just to indulge myself a little. Then a long breath, while I slowly turned to sit and brought the boring businessman back out to see if his life could still be salvaged.

"Oh, my," I said as if dazed, "how embarrassing—did I miss, er, was I gone long?"

A few minutes later, I had received introductions all around to a baker, brick-hauler, dock loaders and sailors, mothers, seamstresses and laundresses. Even the guardsman Beirill checked me over amiably, as I resisted the urge to touch my face. He patted his whistle and warned me to let the trained professionals handle the job from now on, and I agreed I would. I returned to the table to finish discussing the idea of a tab with Noudhal, while a part of my mind chose which names to remember, others to forget. Incredibly, it seemed folks were accepting what I had done—unusual yes, but not a flicker of suspicion from anyone. Except Keilee; I sensed in her a child as bright as curious. But she didn't know what to make of me—with luck she would live many years before putting two and two together. For the rest of the neighborhood, the chance broke fortunately—I could almost feel the way they would reason in the future. That fellow, Feldspar? Nonsense, I saw him myself—fell in the river.

I left Noudhal with a letter of credit, painfully explained, and promised to return that evening to meet all the regulars. He directed me to my address, just the next right beyond his inn as it happened; an alley adjoined us back to back. I walked up the quiet, surprisingly clean street to the front door and produced my key, along with a letter from the precinct scribe who had arranged the sale.

The Twelfth of the Dolphin, 2002 ADR

Citizen Simith,

In accordance with your instructions, I have secured the lease on a very suitable domicile in the northern quadrant of the city, just overlooking The Boards. This sturdy two-and-one-half floor house is well-appointed, spacious, secure, and an excellent opportunity for the aspiring professional business man such as yourself. The neighborhood is a family one, located in the rustic and entertaining docks quarter of the old northern district, actually within a short walk of the Tepid River, affording a view of mysterious Old Cryss, site of the supposed horrors and lawless men whose stories no doubt thrilled you as a boy! Rest assured, however, that no danger from the abandoned Older City threatens your home; the Overlord's agents avow no one lives there, due to sanitary hazards predating more recent advances. At all events, the City guards are always within call, day or night, and pride themselves in responding to any warning bell sounded in the precinct within ten minutes.

I looked up and down the row of houses facing each other, small, dingy, identical. Poor people on all sides, by my standards at least frighteningly poor. And the quality of the city guards I already knew first-hand—I felt no fear that they would ever be on the scene when truly needed. Ten minutes in my business was an eternity. I insisted on a neighborhood like this, so that I could be free to come and go. And I also wanted workers around me, because they would be more likely than others to take their sleep. Unlocking the door, I stepped into the antechamber of Simith's new home.

Being next to The Boards, your home is in a still-active port neighborhood, where the sounds of merchant traffic and sailor-songs add a quaint touch to the neat, uniform houses of your street. The solid wall at the end of your row was erected to facilitate the off-loading of cargo, especially barrels, from the docks. It serves as an effective barrier against the actual intrusion of sea traffic onto your street, and makes it quiet as well.

I laughed aloud, in my solitude, to read the man squirm and trample the truth. I might have told him I was going to take the place at once, but I didn't want to seem too eager. A ship had pulled into quay just as I left the tavern. Even inside I could hear the rumble of rolling wood, the shouts and curses of the crew as they bashed their goods around on the docks beyond the wall. The racket was startling; it sounded to me as if they were competing to break the most containers during the walloping process. Perhaps they had a prize at stake. But it served my purpose. Elves don't need to sleep unless ill or hurt—but most of them love to, all the same. Any folks who could sleep through that thunder would never awaken at the passing of the lightest feet in the city.

The Grog's Lees tavern around the corner actually abuts your house-row at the mutual privy areas, and this too serves to deaden the pleasant roister of the sailor folk who frequent it. It is of course most convenient to your own custom as well, and will certainly facilitate your early welcome into this neighborhood. The other businesses of the immediate area are of completely approbationary nature, and of no concern in terms of references. Droke Staveshaver, for example, represents the finest in Cryssigensian barrelmakers as his family has been in the business for over three hundred years. The presence of such established and respectable businessmen as Droke contributes to the value of your home and the safety and comfort of the precinct. Your other neighbors will no doubt introduce themselves soon.

Soon indeed, I thought as I perused the downstairs dining room, study and kitchen—none of which I had ever used before—and then climbed the central stair to the second level. Droke had been one of those taking my hand after my half-intentional rescue; strapping fellow, fiery red hair and I saw on his worn work tunic a bright crimson button. The others had all since been replaced, but there was no mistaking the original. Droke Staveshaver was a House man then, low level or he'd have been given a new suit, but not out of membership or he wouldn't dare to keep the button. And the bricklayer, Giurid I think it was, wore a blue sash for a belt around his waist. Colors like that could never be copied. The stealthic inside me wondered if the day would come, when one House asked me to steal from his rival the best guarded secret in the empire. And I wondered, in turn, if I would say yes.

I poked into the first bedrooms upstairs, to the left, and thought they were too big. When I realized these must be for guests, or servants, I shook my head smiling. Back to the south of the staircase, the entire half-level was taken up by my own sleeping chamber. Now I laughed—I could practice fencing in here if I moved a few chairs. Come to think of it, there must have been a dozen of those in the house; did people visit one another at all hours? I sat in one and heard the relative silence on this end of my new house. Then my eye wandered back to the agent's letter in my hand.

No description of your home could be complete without mention of the amazing sanitation system provided for this district by the wisdom of His Eminence and Radiance, the Overlord Toll'k'r over four hundred years ago. Your home, like every one in this district, is supplied with a faultless and extraordinary system for the removal of waste. Simply enter the clean, secluded privy room on either floor, deposit whatever undesirable waste you may wish, and leave. Within moments, the detritus is miraculously taken out of your life forever! No more wading through filth, risking new clothing and one's delicate sensibilities in the distasteful traffic of the common herd; the cleanness this system brings to the neighborhood is a major point of its attractiveness and value, and I'm sure you'll agree after only a short stay. One warning: it is recommended that no one ever be in the privy-room at the stroke of midnight on a full lower moon. The wisdom of the builders no doubt requires this simple precaution.

There was more in the letter, but this I had to see for myself. I ran to the back-side of the house and on the wall, just to one side of the stair landing there stood a small door, like a closet. Inside, I saw a place to sit with the hole you would expect—here, in my house, a garderobe like a castle! I sniffed strongly but nothing came to me. Too good to be true? I tested it out, and my butt twitched every second I sat there. I almost couldn't produce anything but after laughing harder and harder I finally relaxed. Hitching my breeks, I checked again for any scent—nothing. Incredible!

I examined the boards of the seat and the back wall, and finally the roof above the seat. Suitable, might be the best place to insert the hatch. But that was some way into the future: chimneys, windows, the roof itself and any basement space still had to be inspected. Within three days, I estimated, I could make this place secure and able to house the man with endless faces. The marked crate from my old warehouse should arrive tomorrow. Tonight, it only remained to frequent the bar and meet more locals.

The knock on the door brought me to myself instantly. I expected no one, and my home was not nearly ready for any number of people Feldspar had met in his adventures. I saw the thick bolt and he urged me to throw it closed, then flee. With an effort, I reminded myself that no stealthic lived here; I put on my stone-seller's face and opened. Keilee stood on the first step, arms akimbo and a face filled with future misery.

"Well hello there," I said as blandly as I could manage, "won't you come in and sit? I seem to have plenty of chairs."

"I am to apologize, citizen Simith, for the trouble I caused you today." Keilee recited well enough, but I took a quick glance up and down the street to see if there was another audience. "I am to offer to work for you all of next week—" clever urchin!-"that is, if you need me." Ah, too greedy there.

"I am just glad that you are well. As for work, well, ahm…" I tried to imagine some smooth answer, a chore that would derail her natural curiosity. No use—I saw the intelligence in her face, could practically feel the energy coursing through her slim frame, and felt helpless to lie. Covering for my own confusion, I turned back into the house and waved vaguely at the furniture in my study. Keilee climbed up into a pillowed armchair and her hips nearly disappeared. I sat on a wooden one next to her and let my eyes wander as if I were thinking of chores rather than a solution to the problem of her presence. She kicked her feet and pretended not to be interested in every facet of the room. How did her parents put up with her every hour? Could anyone be so foolish as to ignore such a bright spark? No wonder she got in trouble.

"I need… say, are you hungry?" I said before I could think. Keilee blinked back at me—at least I had surprised her. "Yes, I feel hungry—the fish stew, em, notwithstanding. Shall we see what I have—why, of course I have nothing!"

I walked with her back to the kitchen, though I knew I had left no instructions with the agent regarding food. I ate very little myself, but that would never do now that I would be normal. The cupboards were bare, and I faced Keilee with a seed sprouting in my mind. "Perhaps you could shop for me?"

"Me?" Keilee was honestly stunned, which made us even. Obviously no one had entrusted her with a task so important. I warmed to the argument.

"Why not? I'm sure you are aware of all the grocers, who has the finest meat, and, em, flour, things like that."

"I do!" she crowed, then subsided a bit, "but then, I don't have any money."

"Oh that," I said dismissively, and drew out a handful of coins from my sash. Time for another honesty test. I laid a row of silver on the cutting counter, followed by two gold. "Now, I want you to select a good variety of things; spices as well as, well, flour and you know, things you can cook a meal with… hire the boys at the grocers to carry it all back here, can you arrange that?" Keilee's mouth fell open as she thought of fellows twice her age who would be following her and the money. "Perhaps your sister can help you pick out some things?"

"She's at temple, they were all called to a big meeting." Oho—the Stargazers were always in the thick of any developments in the city, and something in my gut twinged. Another reason to visit the inn tonight—I might get the signal of another patron to hire me.

"Well then, you will have to make the important decisions on your own."

Keilee was thoroughly engaged in the idea of bossing her neighbors with money. She eyed the coins and hesitated. I prompted her, saying, "You bring back whatever you don't spend, I will tip the carriers."

That was enough for her—she swept the entire pile into her hands, not large enough to carry them hidden, and stared at the treasure. It was probably as much as her father made in half a year, not that he'd be paid in coin anyway. I was tempting her sorely, but she knew it. Looking up, then around at the kitchen, she said, "You don't know how to cook, do you?"

Another lie I could not tell. "I tend to eat in the inns most often."

"I can cook. I help mother all the time."

"Do you want to cook for me?" I asked with a sour jangle in my heart. Keilee thought about it, then nodded. "Well, we shall try it out," I said trying to sound doubtful instead of afraid. "Not breakfast, thanks, I'll manage on my own for that. But dinner, if your parents allow you—it might be best if I drop by and speak to them."

"They won't mind!" she cried almost desperately. "I have to work for you anyway, and they—they will know where I am!" I laughed at that and nodded. "Indeed, but I shall stop in tonight and check with them to be certain."

"You just want to meet my sister," she accused. I hadn't considered that, and indeed it wasn't so at all.

"I'm sure she is a very, ahm, good person," I temporized, and my reluctance was still the truth.

Since I saw her temple badge, I reflected that 'Lashi' probably had some miraculous power, and might have used it without knowing. The higher priestesses had the ability to enchant others to do their bidding—they said some could make one fall in love. Keilee's sister might be learning something of that ability, and in her desperate need for help triggered me to action. Until I knew better, I wanted to be circumspect around her. And her little sister. I really had not expected Simith to get himself in so much trouble; that was supposed to be Feldspar's job.

Keilee took her dismissal with eagerness, running off to shop as fast as she could with her hands clutched together on the treasure at her waist. I rubbed my hair with one hand, then closed the door and went upstairs to prepare for the tavern. By then it would be night, and holding off Feldspar would be more difficult than ever.

⊕ ⊕ ⊕

Simith had never been in a tavern before. Of course, *I* had, dozens of times while searching for information and making contact with my patrons. But it was always in another guise—the ancient beggar if I didn't expect to stay too long, the fencing bravo for higher class establishments (or when I was bored). Three or four others I deployed with some frequency just to keep the bards unsure who was picking up the clues they laid down. But Simith had always been such a nonentity—I used to resort to him only in a tearing rush, or on the way between costume-caches.

Now I stood at the center of the bar, hearing my good name praised up and down as a dozen local sturdies freely drank and spoke about—what else?—politics. I couldn't take one step towards Tambouri Shai as she sang over by the corner. Any minute she might launch into the song or catchphrase that served as my signal, but I was helpless to respond, or even show too much interest. Part of me tried to scratch up an excuse for a stone-seller to be more supportive of the arts, while another part struggled to keep up the bland pretence of Simith's interest in the election of the next Overlord. And underneath it all, Feldspar grumbled for his freedom, ruining my recall.

"-wheat nor corn for a month-"

"-for a single bolt, and worsted at that—"

"-now he'll face trial—"

Assuredly, life in the city was walking about on three legs, without our dear Overlord. No bricks, people daring to sell outside their customary precinct, everyone running out of supplies. I'd heard the same drone in every tavern of the city for five months at least. And if we had an Overlord tomorrow, in another month he'd be blamed for everything that went wrong. I nodded whenever someone paused long enough to require it, and murmured some sympathetic question to the Blue house brick-hauler Giurid, just to keep him going. All the while I tried to hone in on Tambouri and her song: any verse, any chorus, could have the changed lyric that held my cue. She sang *The Lay of Argens*, celebrating our empire's founder and his deeds of millennia ago:

Star and sea, first to be...
Argens First One, wrote anew history's tome, wrought all things well
A slice of sun, the southern run...
Light to world's gloam, brought day to darkest hell, the rustic people free
A land, a home, 'cross sky and foam...
Conquered desert and dell, son of the Three, fought scale and won
Struggle 'gainst demons fell, their secrets forced to tell...
A palace stands eternally, his empire begun, when he dared to roam

I was lucky in more ways than one, as I kept gazing over at her in snatches. No man could question another staring at Tambouri

Shai—her figure was fine, it was true, but how many could tear themselves away from her emerald eyes? And she sang like a captive mockingbird; I paid ticket money to hear her in the concert halls, whereas most of the other bards in the city were just so-so, she was one of the very best. But she sang the epic of Argens straight up, no changes. I thought I caught her looking us all over, trying to spot someone in particular. Maybe she was hoping to meet the beggar again, he was a fairly well-known contact among the singers. She'd never met Simith. If only I could get closer.

But the sailor just in from Cesmir asked me about my business, and I had to give him some attention.

"Ceramic, mainly," I said, "and sometimes lime." I let my face shine with that pedantic eagerness to talk on and on about common stone, and the magic of boredom wove its usual spell for me. I almost chuckled in the man's face. Then it occurred to me I should make up some business to have, in case someone asked. Simith had never done a lick of work before—he just picked up money at the bank and disappeared from public view. Real life was becoming complicated. The quarries and types of stone I knew well, but I had no idea really who would want to buy building supplies. Might be fun.

Now Giurid was on about crime, which meant the subject would very soon come around to me. From the corner of my eye I watched him—the man was strong as an ox and always seemed to lead with his sash. Proud of the Blue, the belt that declared his house; I wondered why. The sash-knot was so tight, I could tell the man slept in his clothes. The way he stood with a thumb hooked in it was comic, until he called Feldspar a thief. Something inside me growled at that, and more, at the whole charade. It was well after dark, time to be out and about on the rooftops and in the culverts. But I had no commission since returning the Fire Grip's gavel, and I could sense Tambouri held my next one, right on the top of her tongue.

"A thief's a thief," a thin man insisted, confident that the person he spoke of wasn't close enough to pour a tankard down his shirt. Someone else jumped to my defence, and while I like watching other folks fighting, this was getting me nowhere closer to the bard. Pretty ironic if they lost me a job scrapping over my honor.

27

Bless the woman's good sense, she changed tunes before a fight broke out. My heart leapt as I recognized it, *Trekelny's Ballad*. The rumors said he had always wanted a song written about him, though I'd never knew anyone who claimed to have seen him either. The crowd favorite about a great stealthic's exploits, that was the beginning of a clue, one way the bards could let Feldspar know he was wanted.

The moon's shifting shadow was his friend,
He climbed the tower walls
All through the temple he did wend,
A' glide past guarded halls...

That settled it, I had to get a word with Tambouri. While seeking an opening to visit her corner I temporized, asking about the ceremony that would take place in two days to elect the new Overlord. Normally I wouldn't pay two silver bits for the information, I hate politics. But I couldn't guide the conversation to a close unless I participated; I bought a final round to cap it off.

There was a lot of clap about the various sects, vying with each other for supremacy now that the cult of Argens Demonbender was outlawed. The highest preachers, together with the guild leaders, House Cups, and the surviving feudal magnates, would gather to vote on the successor to the Overlord.

"And that will happen... ah, the day past tomorrow?" I asked, trying not to sound as if I were in a hurry.

"Aye, second day from now's the Ides. In the arena, I hear."

"The arena!" I blurted out, honestly surprised. "Why not the church, then?"

"'s'Closed, you fool," a woman muttered, and I noted immediately her iron-hard arms around the drinking cup.

"What Delith means," said Giurid, "is the Demonbender temple's closed. Ever since the stubby carker took over, you canna' worship where you would anymore." Folks buzzed a bit about what the emperor had outlawed, and I nodded, though I was frankly more angry about the sect he had revived.

"So," I said trying to look confused, "that's where the investiture ceremony for the new Mark, the Overlord WOULD have taken place, but now..."

"Now, they canna' agree!" Giurid rejoined gleefully. "All the preachers, Hopeforgers, Stargazers, the Cryssians, those new ones, the name of that healer used to be outlawed…"

Here I could not stop myself from answering. "Telhol," I said, and while my eyes took in his thanks, my stomach lurched with shame and anger.

Yula the First could do as he liked, for my vote. Outlaw slavery, ban the drug trade, take away lands from some and give them to others. His right, if he won the war. Those who complained were likely just beholden to the losers. I never thought about politics more than I had to. And besides, it just created more work for me, from the newly-powerful who wished to keep their seats and from the freshly disgraced who yearned to win them back. Both were in the market for the best talent in the city. I would miss the gladiatorial games, but I never went in for drugs as I needed to keep the mind and body sharp. Some good, some bad—the emperor's edicts did not ruin my life. All but one. He brought back the worship of Telhol, and for that I could never forgive the stubby northern bastard. So his representative wasn't going to make the vote, waylaid in the hills? Good. Damn him to hell and gone—he took my former life from me.

I couldn't think about that now. The folks were all happy, for the moment, and I had a chance to approach Tambouri. She sat unsinging, just shaking her head slightly at the roisterous crowd and their impolitude. I almost chuckled myself, thinking what fine and respectful receptions she received in the amphitheater, the crowns of ivy she had won in previous years. Right now Tambouri Shai mistakenly believed she would never return to the Grog's Lees. But then, she hadn't spoken to me yet.

Even as I stepped next to her I could see her gaze slide past, politely nodding her head but still searching. For the beggar, I guessed, though she thought it a lost cause—like all my other personae, he was noticeable, to the nose even before the eye. I bowed and also avoided her gaze, because a fellow could get lost in those emerald pools and I needed to keep my focus.

"Mistress Shai," I began, giving her a title beyond her station. Her lips curled up with the flattery and she looked more directly at me. "I am so very pleased that our little, em, gathering here should

29

be graced by your unexpected presence. I have often heard you in the concert halls, if I may say so."

"You are very kind, sir," she murmured while taking a sip of wine. Her lithe frame as she turned, the way the cloud of her red hair stayed so firm and vibrant, the lilt of her voice even in speaking. She paired the beauties of sight and sound. And what did I offer? Only the life's blood of her calling—information. Poor woman, it wasn't going to be a fair contest. I could tell she still expected nothing, even having sung the clue-song. But that changed in an instant when I gave the first pass-word.

"I was particularly thrilled to hear you sing of that great stealthic, Trekelny." Her green eyes snapped to look at me directly, still guarded but with the smile dropped. "Do you suppose," I drawled quietly, "that there is a better stealthic in all the Lands?"

It was her turn now, and I could see the lovely bard suspected the truth at last—at least, as much of the truth as she could understand. She pretended to consider a moment, and then replied, "Some would say that Feldspar of Cryssigens is as accomplished."

"At least," I returned immediately, "he is nearby."

That was the way of it. The patrons called in the bards when they had need to speak with Feldspar. The bards worked in tavern and on street-corner, by the docks and outside the arena, singing the ballad of Trekelny's deed or inserting a mistaken phrase to another song as if by accident. And soon or late, one of them would hear from a young elven maiden, or the ripe beggar, perhaps a preacher of Argens Hopeforger or an out-of-work sailor, and the ritual words would be exchanged. Agents of the famous Feldspar, scattered throughout the city, everyone buzzed with the knowledge and not one of them suspected the truth. Cryssigens was above all a city of display, of public delight in the attention one could draw, the connections and family and power one boasted of openly. What man would be mad enough to hide, to take on disguises and act like someone else? Even now, with her eyes fully upon me, trying to drink in every mundane detail of my completely normal appearance, I felt safe from Tambouri Shai. The beggar she expected, even if stretched on the rack, would be a full two inches shorter than Jonn Simith; how I manage that I will never tell a soul. She was no fool, and would remember the

Grog's Lees, the seller of stone, for all future messages. But the truth eluded her, and that was just as I liked it.

It was now my turn to complete the transaction, by discovering the patron and validating her commission. "That song—where did you sing it last?"

"It was in the temple of the Stargazers," Tambouri returned in measured tones, "in the room of the High Priestess W'Starrah Altieri herself."

So that was my next patron, the infamous Lavender Lady, an ambitious elven noble of whom I heard many things, not least of which that she aspired to great influence in the present controversy. I was afire to know how I might be of service, and Feldspar rankled at any delay now the news was out. Just one detail to attend to.

Reaching into my sash, I produced a small flecked stone polished to a smooth cabochon on the top, flat beneath. "I thank you once again, mistress, for the pleasure of your conversation nearly as much as the beauty... of your song." With a small flourish, I placed the gem in her palm, feeling with my thumb the small number I had scratched on the underside. Tambouri's eyes lit on my meager tip—a nail-sized gem of unremarkable appearance, the sort sometimes used for currency in the outer towns, worth perhaps two or three silver pieces. But it was in fact a piece of feldspar, that the common folk keep for luck; her gaze rose to me with hunger, barely concealed in public. With this, she could return at once to the Stargazer temple, and claim it was by her doing that Feldspar would come. The gemstone was her key to a large commission; hundreds of silver pieces unless I missed my guess, provided I showed up to validate it. And I surely would—now that the clues were given, I could feel the spirit of the stealthic pressing on me, and my time was short.

I returned to the bar, gave them all a final toast, signed my debt-chit and left, trying not to look like a man in a hurry. The songstress caught my eye with a gentle finger-salute on my way out, and I smiled in return a bit more confidently than a mere admirer would. Then again, I felt quite sure that on her next visit to the Grog's Lees, I would have no trouble gaining Tambouri Shai's attentions. As long as she thought me just a conduit to the great man, all well and good.

It was dark as a cave in the neighborhood, with neither moon yet up and no street-lanterns on this late. But elves see well under the stars. It was but two turns of the block back to my street, and consumed with thoughts of the upcoming commission, I let my guard down. Just at the last corner, with my house only four rods away, I made out three forms already splayed to each side of me on the deserted corner. Blast the luck—I was being mugged.

I quickly scanned them, burly for elves, each one wielding a short blade or a tight hard club. They were confident yet alert, and the hulking leader had scars so deep and pocked I could make them out despite the darkness. A former gladiator, I'd bet everything I had on me, which I was about to lose anyway.

"A bit late, citizen," the big leader chuckled. "A bit late for walking the streets alone."

Another unfair fight. Feldspar could make short work of any trio of street-toughs. But they would scream on the way down, and I couldn't be sure of killing all three before the guards came. The kind of questions that followed would mean the end for Jonn Simith. I let my mouth hang open and took two steps away from the leader, while I thought furiously what to do. I could most likely outdistance them too, no bows. But that was even worse—three witnesses to a helpless merchant who ran like an alley-hound and dodged better than a swallow. Feldspar, of course, didn't care a fig for my identity, nearly lost several times already today. He pressed to begin the contest, and I had to wrestle him back from starting up.

"Leave me alone!" I growled, and the robber laughed, thinking I meant him.

"Surely, citizen, just after ye's paid the toll. Get his attention, Farlo."

The one closest to behind me snapped his club against the back of my head. I had noted him, of course, but I couldn't let on that a merchant rube had the awareness of a hawk, the reflexes of an eyra. I lurched into a small, submissive bow, and took the blow glancing on my skull. It stung, but I've had worse. I over-reacted to the tap, falling to my knees and gasping as if nearly unconscious. Reaching quickly into my sash under cover of my fall, I grabbed the remaining small coins I hadn't given to Keilee—why weren't her hands bigger!

I let them drop dramatically to the cobbles at my knees, six silver and four bits.

"Pu-please! Do not hurt me, sirs!" Too late, I thought I could have added a drunken slur. Ah well.

Farlo kicked me out of the way, and I had to take most of the blow on my ribs or else it would have looked suspicious. Stooping, he scraped up the coins while the others stood looking tough indeed. I crouched, no threat; things were going very well.

"Six and four, Barkarr," he said after counting twice. I tried to look as scared as I could without over-acting. The leader scanned me with his arms akimbo, and I started to smell something wrong in the delay. Or maybe he just felt like hurting someone tonight.

"He's got more," he declared, and stepped a little closer to where I groveled on my knees. "Shake him down, boys."

Very bad. There were certain items I always carried, and some could not be easily explained away. With a shock and stifled curse, I remembered my last coin, in a secret pouch—in almost four years I had never had to use it. The stealthic in me chortled, but I kept him down a few moments longer as the pair closed in. I took several slaps and another clubbing from Farlo, who was very much in love with hitting me behind the head. I made frantic flailing gestures while I babbled for mercy, unloading the inner pockets they'd have been suspicious to find secreted inside my sash. Some more feldspar gems fell to the street, a bit of paper, my key, and the leather pouch that looked empty. But I only had two arms, and they patted me down anyway.

"What's this then?" the third one exclaimed with an oath, feeling the twin sticks inside my belt at the spine. Yanking up my tunic he extracted them, two thin hafts joined by several links of chain.

"That!" I said in a high-pitched voice, cutting off any comment, "My measuring cleat, gentlemen—please, no more, I will give you everything, please. It serves me to estimate orders—I deal in stone, bringing pallets to those who need them."

"These?" Farlo cried, grabbing them away and letting one end dangle down, coming very close to wielding the weapon as he stared at it. I moved in and gently took them from him to demonstrate. This part, I had rehearsed before—perhaps there was some hope.

"You see the marks along the side? We measure stone in hand-widths, so there are just four on each side of the cleat, each stick, yes?" I showed him with the width of my own hand. Farlo nodded, frowning with concentration. "And the two sticks together end to end," now I was down on the street hands and knees with it, holding them against the square cobbles that lined all the streets in Cryssigens, "they add up to the exact length of a cobble-square. That's a basic measure of stone too, the cobble-square, every street in the city is like it whether it be lime, or shale or sandstone—"

"Yes, alright." Barkarr was losing interest, and Feldspar got in under my guard, twitting him where it wasn't needed.

"So you see, I can use it to measure partial orders—like that corner piece over there, and half-diagonals, whatever the client requires—"

"Shut up, you little nit, or we'll dump you in the river."

"Why the chain, though?" Farlo asked, and now I had to answer.

"Ah that!" I exclaimed with avid gaiety, though I was furious with the risk-lover inside. "Suppose you must measure a length around a corner, like so," and I stooped to the pavement to put one stick along each edge of a cobble's angle. "The chain gives me just a little room, as when the stone is bulky, you know? And then again, sometimes the angle is not square, so these marks here—"

"I said shut up!" roared Barkarr, and his men all jumped looking about for the guard. That sealed it right there—Feldspar had made him lose his temper, so now someone would have to pay in pain. That was the way of scum like this—and frankly, the stealthic wrestling for control could not have been happier. But I was determined to hang onto my identity at all costs, and I managed to make him stifle beneath the flesh.

I might have escaped with a beating—and flexed and dodged to avoid the worst of it—but the third thug had picked up the pouch and felt inside it. Damn the luck, damn it straight to all the hells below.

"Hey boss," the man said, and everyone turned to watch him slowly finger one more coin out of the pouch. He held it up in the dim light for all of us with elven sight to see, "He's got one more coin here—big and heavy, who has a coin made of iron?"

"You idiot," Barkarr rasped with his eyes on fire, "that's silversteel."

One coin, kept for emergencies, of a kind not minted in the last millennium, and worth more than two hundred silver pieces now. The three looked up at me and I saw my death-warrant on all their faces. This was the level of wealth that summoned the guards, that reported the crime and gave descriptions, and put the law on the muggers until they were caught. They could never let someone of my resources live.

Feldspar was so happy he almost capered in spite of me, but I was still determined to fight for Simith's life. I ruthlessly put down any effort to say something witty or brave, held my eyes as if terrified, kept backing up with legs that wanted instead to shift, maneuver, attack.

But as the gang closed in, I let Feldspar have my hands.

The third one took a swing with his cutlass as Farlo raised the club for another strike. I dropped to my knees as if begging for mercy, shouted "No, please! I beg you, help!" and let one end of the *noun-chakas* swing free in a sharp circle that rapped the sword-wielder's wrist. Numbed, his fingers released automatically and the blade fell to the street. I went prone in abasement, shooting out both legs a bit faster than one would expect; it tripped Farlo behind me just as he swung that blasted club. He half-fell over my thighs and into Barkarr, who swore and threw him hard onto the curb, where he would be a bit stunned. I scrambled to my feet still yelling—for if they meant to kill me they could no longer expect me to keep quiet—and half-ran, half-dove to one side, right next to Farlo as if by accident.

"No please! Help! Help me!" I pretended to get the measuring cleat tangled, my fingers caught between the sticks and the chain. I made as if to throw it down with either hand, faster and faster. The two sticks began to swing in alternation with increasing speed as I shouted and stumbled. When I straightened out just over the rising Farlo, one haft happened to slap into the back of his head with a very satisfying crunch. He sighed and went back down—my body blocked most of the view. *There!* The stealthic shouted triumphantly, and I suggested to him that perhaps he was at last having a good time.

Before he could consider that properly, Barkarr was upon me.

"You scum, what did you do to Farlo with that thing?" This was not a happy pass; the leader was too thoroughly aroused to let me live no matter what, and I was coming to feel the same way about him.

35

He lifted his blade, then swung a roundhouse at my head—clever. I couldn't dodge the punch without giving myself away, and it made me see more stars than the sky normally holds.

"Puh-agh! Please, sir, this is only a tool—here, take it!" I cried, and as he came with the expected follow-up thrust, I shoved my *noun-chakas* out at him, a hand on either haft, trying to surrender them. I neatly caught the incoming strike in the center link of chain, and then screamed to see the point so close to my chest. Twisting as if in dazed panic, I quickly turned my arms in a half circle, lodging the tempered steel chain around the point of his pig-iron blade. Barkarr's arm was stronger than a tree limb, so the weakest point in the contest had to give. The blade snapped off at the hilt and I screamed again, feigning total surprise at the result I had trained hours to achieve.

The third bravo approached holding out his sword hilt-first with his left hand. Ignoring it with an oath, Barkarr punched me from his hilted fist, so that metal and bone both rattled my ribs. Nothing I could do but take it, though I tensed my muscles against the shot. Balls of Astor, he was strong! And not a moment's hesitation in him, definitely a gladiator. Another reason to curse Yula; except for his moralizing, this grunt would still be in the arena where he belonged. He grabbed my neck hard and I could see it coming a mile away; lift and strangle. Dropping my arm, I brought the hafts of the *noun-chakas* up with a half-swing and the force of his lift, directly between his legs. The crushing force on my windpipe eased at once, and as he gasped liquor-breath and spit all over me, we fell backwards together over the body of poor Farlo, a macabre love-trio. I was pinned for now by Barkarr's weight, and he was not going to do much for a moment either. The third man stopped, completely unsure what to do; against my expectation, I heard Farlo moan beneath my shoulders. I had absolutely no choice any more, and started to laugh with all the wheezing half-breaths that the load on my chest allowed.

For a wonder, the guard arrived.

I took back all the mean-spirited things I had been thinking about them earlier; the whistle and tramp of booted feet were sweeter than Shai's song to me now. Barkarr, still gasping, heaved himself up and started to shout something to his fellow; one hand gripped my tunic as if he still meant to finish the job. I squealed, tinged with high-pitched laughter so that I sounded like an escaping piglet, and kicked furiously with both feet the way I imagined a girl would do. My left foot lashed out into his stubbled jaw as he tried to speak, slamming the teeth into the tongue and provoking a blood-specked roar of frustration. Getting all the way up, Barkarr aimed one last kick at me, and I let him score though it nearly broke a rib. Holding one hand to his mouth and still hobbling, he gestured his fellow one way while turning the other.

"Meet at the piazzo?" the lackey said, and Barkarr turned back to swat him so hard on the head he nearly went down. Chastised, the two ran their separate ways. With the guard approaching down The Boards, I quickly scooped up the feldspar gems and my door key, left the rest along with Farlo and hied up the alleyway just as they came in sight down my street. Moving silently I passed them with the houses between us, and slid into the narrow space between my house and the neighboring one, peeking out just as they rounded the corner to the scene of the crime. Three guards, leaving one back at their post—and the tallest, under the lantern, was Beirill. Figured—working a shift for the Fire Grip was probably an extra job for him. Justice never sleeps, especially when he's an elf. I waited until the light faded, then limped quietly to the door and used the key. Only my right foot was not hurting from exertion, bruises, curb-scrapes or that demon-cursed club.

In the foyer I stubbed my right foot on a large crate that had been left in the darkness. Stumbling over it to the floor, I reasoned that now I was even all over. Every part of me I could think of hurt. I gingerly rose and my head swam from the throbbing lump on the back of my head. I hopped towards the living room, and my bruised ribs shouted at every landing. I wondered where civilized folk kept the lantern-matches. Groping hurt my fingers, stepping made my muscles shout, and tripping over chairs barked my shins in any spot the thugs had missed. The matches were reasonably close to where I guessed, but instead of a lantern on the table I could only find some sheets of paper. I lit them at one corner and as the room flared to view around me I saw burning fragments of the property scribe's closing:

In short, Mister Simi... sure... vely home completely to your satis ... a pleasure to be of serv... will eagerly place... your disposal if ... may require it.

Just inside the living room entry hung a nice lantern, perfect for lighting a dark house and easy to use by anyone who knew where in the Hells Below it was hiding. After I lit it, I patted out the burnt letter; only the closing still survived.

May the Flame Eternal Burn Bright in Your New Home,
Thalek Poronar, Property Scribe

An eternal flame—might be good to have one around here. I looked back to the foyer by lantern light; the route appeared absurdly easy now. I laughed and it hurt, and I laughed louder because it hurt. Setting down the lantern, I looked around and felt the silence for a while. Then I deliberately picked up one of the overturned chairs and bashed it against the wall repeatedly. The pain in my sides kept shrieking but I didn't stop until the legs splintered.

I felt a bit better—my house, I could do as I liked with everything in it. I chuckled aloud to the shadows around me—even in the warehouse I had never been so free to relax. Of course if I wrecked a chair every day, people would eventually start to wonder.

I returned to the foyer, hung the lantern and came back to the crate. It contained my things from the warehouse, and on top lay the second door key, now returned by the property scribe to conclude our relationship. There was no key in existence for the lock on the crate itself—I picked it, and threw back the lid. It was all there. But first, I had to get clean.

In the kitchen I laved water over all of me, gradually disrobing as I did. Naked and wet I shivered a bit against the chill, and grinned at the bruises I had all over. So far, being a normal person did not seem worth the trouble. But time to consider that later. Without a stitch on, I returned to the foyer, and even though no one could see I turned the lantern down to a flicker to better prepare.

The clothing bundle was last, after I had strapped the extras I usually carried to my wrists, back and ankles. Tight-fitting black breeches and shirt, a seven-holstered belt for the *noun-chakas* and other tools, a backpack so small it looked like a flap below my shoulders. The gloves rolled on halfway up each arm. Then the hooded mask, black and anonymous, yet carrying the impression of a much more aquiline face, nose, brow. The supple leather fit like skin and carried no mouth, but had a small slit to allow speaking. There was a tiny tuft of blonde hair showing from one side, a final bit of deception.

I tied on the mask and Feldspar was at last free again. My pains of the day, the exhaustion, confusion, even the wounds themselves simply disappeared. Only normal people like Jonn Simith suffered those. I closed the crate and relocked the hasp. Sliding out the kitchen door into the alley, Feldspar headed for the temple of the Stargazers.

⊕ ⊕ ⊕

The moons were up now, which created some interesting moments at street crossings where guards were stationed. But elevation resolved them, as always. People hardly ever look up; and in the streets and alleys, shadows prevailed. I moved across the upper city with ease, quiet but for the sounds of the taverns and a few returning patrons; once I heard the distant echo of applause from the theater and felt a tingle of pleasure. But the temple quarter, closer to the sea-cliffs, was quiet. I could hear the ocean below clearly as I slid over the wall and into the Stargazer compound.

This was to be a study-night; Feldspar never confronted a patron he didn't know about. The Lavender Lady took no pains to hide herself—why should she! Still, her motives were a mystery to me and I needed to scout them out. Not that I cared about her politics one way or another; but I refuse to be surprised if I can avoid it. So tonight I would watch and wait.

The church of Argens Stargazer emphasizes beauty, future-sight and of course the power of love. The temple grounds were more of a park where the holy men and women could counsel their followers in private. Exotic shrubs, lilac and willow trees and wide benches dotted the rolling lawn; shadows contended with each other to darken the most space. I could have hidden a company of soldiers anywhere.

I passed by more than one coupling, tossing and sighing in the kind of delight that can only be found here. I shook my head and chuckled as I slipped along. Go down into the eastern quarter by the outer gates and pay a woman perhaps fifty silver, and that engaged a prostitute, for sex. But here, one handed over a thousand silver or more, and the preacher or priestess thus dallied with brought enlightenment. From over by the gate, one slunk away half-resolved never to return. From here, one left with head held high, a good son or daughter of the church—though just as sweaty and tired, it seemed to me. And they returned as soon as they had the money.

The guards here were paid not to give too much attention; getting to the tower of the preachers was child's play. I found a good spot atop a shaded gazebo with a vantage on Altieri's windows as well as the tower entrance, and settled in to watch. She was in her chambers, and at first I saw servants stirring with bundles—outfits and accessories, I guessed. The area behind the tower was a hive of work, even in the dead of night. Wardrobes and tapestries getting washed, fresh supplies brought in. Of course—the new Overlord would be seated before the sunset after next, and the celebrations at the Stargazer temple must be second to none, if they were to retain their status with the city's elite. I thought about the bacchanal they must have planned and my mouth got wet. Maybe the fencer could wrangle his way inside.

As time passed in silence the scent of the place stole over me—even in mid-winter flowering plants bloomed everywhere, carefully chosen to emphasize foresight and heighten perception. I looked across the grounds to the small church-school and my mind stole back to childhood, when I had received instruction from the kindly preachers in all the subjects they thought important. Literacy I owed to them, as well as more knowledge of navigation than I ever wanted, some herbal lore, physical exercise, tenets of faith in Argens (with liberality to those who were called differently), and most of all exposure to the arts of performance. The chorus and drama were more important to the Stargazers than any other sect of Argens. Here I received my early training as well as introductions to several actors of the day, which proved useful, when I started on my own.

With an effort, I shook myself back to attention: W'starrah's cupola was still buzzing without pause or resolution. Yes, perhaps the purple dress, I thought—how difficult could it be. One priestess in particular, I recalled, who taught the students well, so beautiful and kind. I groped for her name—every child simply called her "priestess" as if she were the only one there. But she had encouraged everyone to try the theater, in children's roles and standing with the chorus, and of course I fell in love with her. She always wore a red tunic-dress with a white border; I wondered what had become of her these past two decades, and whether she looked the same or had

40

aged. An elf never knows when the aging process will stop; for the clerics of the Stargazer temple, youth and looks were more important than elsewhere.

I almost missed W'starrah Altieri, beautiful as she was. The tower door opened to release three shapes, and if not for the enormous black in front, I would have taken them for workers. But Altieri's Nubian bodyguard, towering well over seven feet, was impossible to mistake. So the second figure must be the Lavender Lady herself. She was cloaked in darkest indigo, with a wrap for her face; only her eyes and the upper frame of champagne hair showed, along with just hints of the body beneath. And still I hungered, as all men do, at the sight of her. An attendant followed, also cloaked; as I watched them head off the grounds I felt that click of curiosity inside me, and prepared to follow.

W'starrah Altieri, best known of all the Stargazer preachers, dazzling light of Cryssigens society, was traveling practically incognito in the dark of night. Of course, any fool would know that her Nubian would never leave her side, and even from a distance I could tell she was dressed to slay, as for any public occasion. Old habits die hard, for most of us—but certainly she was not trying to advertize her movements tonight. All the better to know them. I slipped down from the gazebo and lagged along behind them into the upper city.

Within two hundred steps I let them distance me, and focused on making sure I wasn't seen. The distinctive scent of jasmine and a spice I could not name was sharp in the night air. Anyway, by then I could tell where they were headed. Down a wonderfully cobbled and decorated way, they moved towards the temple of Argens Hopeforger. Things were going to get difficult—the Hopeforgers were devotees of the light.

I could see the glow hanging over the temple compound long before the outer gates were in direct view. The guards stationed there were fully illuminated by mirror-torches, and their armor shone well enough to double what flame began. As soon as I saw W'starrah and her companions stop there to be passed through, I ducked into an alley and worked around at a sprint to the place where the wall met the sea-cliff. There was a guard there as well, and a torch, but I timed his passing and stood against the wall directly beneath him.

I carefully bent out the arms of the wrist-bow and loaded it with the small parchment packet. I waited until the far end of his walk to cock it, and the click was very small. When he came back, I let him pass, then climbed to the edge of his walk, took careful aim, and let it fly. The packet hit the space just above his head against the end-tower and exploded with a small pop. The guard stopped and looked around, as a cloud of white mist settled around his head.

Talc, of course, is a kind of stone and I had come to know it well; mixed with tobacco ash, it made the cloud smell like pipe-smoke, allaying suspicion and covering the scent of the somnos. The guard sniffed suspiciously, and looked down over the wall to find the offender. I eased onto the walk in plain sight and crouched to wait. In less than a minute, he had gone from woozy to yawning to dead asleep on his feet. I leaped forward and eased him back to sit against the tower, with his spear decorously laid across his lap. Embarrassed, he would feel no need to report his lapse when he woke. So much better than a fight, a possible alarm, and all the attendant mess.

I dropped down into the grassy compound and saw a completely different place. Paved pathways with light-posts, sharp corners with long sight-lines, all devoid of legitimate traffic. Everything pointed towards the enormous temple in the center of the compound, where the edifice to Argens Hopeforger loomed, a hundred well-lit windows facing to all sides. This sect represented the majority of the city's population, and emphasized the vigilance, pride and natural leadership of the First of the First, as Argens was known here.

And this too was familiar to me; tonight was evidently a night for recollection. I worked my way quickly but indirectly across the grounds, diving towards sharply-edged planes of shadow that the lights created in a few selected spots, just as I had done in my youth. After my parents' death I was sent to the church school here as an orphan, for the Hopeforger naturally took care of the helpless and poor. I headed directly towards the school building now, larger and thankfully darkened this late. Under its eaves I traced steps I had used to avoid my teachers and taskmasters scores of times back then. Whenever they caught up with me—which became increasingly rare as I grew to manhood—they dragged me back and taught me basic numbers, and the ways of stonemasonry which some wise person had decided would be my trade. I decided otherwise of course, and ran off to the theater before I turned twenty. For their side, the Hopeforger preachers had not looked for me overlong, and we had agreed to leave it at that.

Now I was within the shadow of the temple itself, moving from a slight culvert to an angle behind the spreading cypress tree, a pair of hiding spots I think no one else has ever discovered. Three tall stories up, I could see the wide windows where the Highforge himself lived, and I was betting that Altieri would meet with no one of lower rank at this time of night. I thought about the layout of that floor from my days serving the priesthood, and guessed the large chamber to the right of his rooms would be the meeting place. I could hide on the roof behind the bell-tower nearby. From there I could see, if not perhaps hear, all that happened. The window overlooked the sea, not the streets, and I bet confidently that it would be brightly lit.

Some nickname me The Spider, and I don't know whether it means the way I can climb sheer stone, or how I unnerve my fellow Elves, who from birth hate and fear all insects. Perhaps a bit of both, I have no objection. Churches are always covered with grand statuary and meaningful patterns, if the builders can afford it. The preachers of the Hopeforger had the money—I have climbed ladders with more trouble. Once or twice I had to put my foot on Argens' stone belt buckle, or his head; that's what made the climb impossible to the people here, and no one looks for me where it's not possible to go.

The guard in the bell-tower was doing his job, which means looking far out over the grounds and even to sea—not paying attention to what might be crouching fifteen feet below him on the gable roof. I clung to the tower in the center of its moon-cast shadow and saw a glittering assembly in the conference chamber, one story higher than me and less than a bowshot away.

I expected to see two very important persons deep in conversation, and instead saw four. Curious indeed. The host, Highforge Z'kammet Hammer loomed from behind the large oak table, well over six feet tall with arms that seemed to embrace the room as he gestured, demanded, interrupted with vigor. Behind his place was a podium with various artifacts of the Hopeforger church. Most I recognized though I never troubled about such things. In the central place now, though, was an unfamiliar sight; a large wooden box inset with gold and silver, each side as long as my forearm. While Hammer spoke he often paced in front of the podium, so it was natural that he should not look at these items, though his guests often did.

Across from him, Priestess Altieri sat with her back half-turned to my view, her cloak removed and a gorgeous purple gown revealed beneath the piles of her light hair. She laughed like a chime and answered the Highforge with a tone that sounded reassuring and knowing, as always. She was soft to his edges, smooth brow to his furrowed, her manner voluble to his venerable; these were old rivals, political opponents and perhaps odd friends. But tonight, they had distinguished guests.

Carnad Mias, the Red House Cup himself, sat in all his hardened corpulent glory on the inside of the table across from Altieri and facing me. Every stitch of his garments, gems and all, showed brilliant red, different shades but all from the genius of the House he chaired. In the entire Southlands, there was no power, no more secure source of wealth, than the genius of the Houses of Color. Across every rank of society, from the fabulously rich down to all but the poorest, there was color. Not faded burgundy or tincts that looked like old scars, but brilliant ruby shades, crimson that made sheets look as thick as the mattresses they covered, blood-hued armor that struck fear into opponents. For the secret of red itself, in whatever material the guilds could devise, to be used on cloth or metal or glass or wood—for red, one must come to the Red House. Hold hat in hand, bow, ask nicely, and of course one must pay. Carnad Mias ran the coterie of those, in several powerful families, who had been entrusted with the secrets of this color: men died every year trying to obtain or sell the methods, and none succeeded.

Carnad sat now listening with a cross expression to the two bantering clerics, but always with an eye to the fourth member of the meeting. As the Highforge ranted on, I also watched that last guest, and I could hardly have been more surprised, or less pleased. The aquiline face atop his slender frame, the shoulder-length shock of chestnut hair, the uniform of a city guardsman he insisted on wearing, decorated only with the brilliant cobalt sash. No one else could carry off the role of the Fire Grip Gaspar Heugen, at once so understated and commanding. He stood at the end opposite Hammer, closest to the door as if he needed to leave at the next pause for breath.

W'starrah Altieri might meet with the head of the Hopeforger church on a whim, just to tease him, or to curry a favor. A threesome including Carnad Mias could mean a conspiracy, something weighty that would change the fate of this or that guild, delay a festival, alter a profit scheme. But the foursome in the room now contained enough power to determine the next Mark of Cryssigens. Thanks to the presence of the highest ranking noble left alive from the war, the elf who stood closest to the Overlord's Throne and served the city as a virtual regent—a high ranking councilor in the Blue House to boot.

And my former employer.

The talk continued, mostly from Hammer as the host, and I couldn't be happier not to hear the details. Politicking makes my stomach hurt. I shifted weight from one leg to the other as I watched, a trick I learned backstage between cameo-roles. Evidently it was more of the same from the Highforge, as Mias' face was not even affecting polite attention any more. The Red Cup stood to pace the floor and speak—always glancing to Heugen as if he dared not show him his back. He drifted to the window to speak in my direction across the rooftop darkness. Elves see well at night, but not from rooms that are lit, and I crouched in the bell-tower's shadow dressed in black; no fear. With a joke of some kind, Mias nodded, turned back to the room and gestured to his ample midriff—Hammer pointed the way to the privy. The Red Cup clapped a hand briefly on W'starrah's shoulder like a companion, then lightly trailed a finger behind her neck as he left, like someone else. She looked after him with a face that smiled winningly on the outside at least. I wondered. No man that rich and powerful should also be so lucky.

Hammer turned then to speak to Heugen, with occasional input from W'starrah, but it was clear the noble would have none of it. The Fire Grip looked positively eager to leave now—when Hammer threw up his hands in frustration, Heugen made an eloquent gesture pointing the way Mias had gone, as if to say that manners dictated he await the return before taking his leave. The conversation quite died at whatever he said; Hammer sat at last while his noble guest remained standing. The Lavender Lady rose and took her goblet to the window, where she looked out over the sea beyond my shoulders, her face filled with… with desire, I decided, but for what I could not tell. The meeting was not going well, yet she seemed far from disappointed with the proceedings. I got a gentle jangle as I looked at her, something beyond the way the sight of her moved any man still breathing. At first I couldn't sort it out, and for an instant I thought of the guard I left sleeping at the wall. Using tobacco had been inspired, made the mist smell like smoke. But that was past, I needed to keep focus.

The Red Cup returned, looking as if he had been frisked by W'starrah's Nubian guard, which was likely true. He bowed to Heugen and resumed his seat, but rose immediately when the Fire Grip announced his departure. One last imprecation from Hammer, politely but firmly cut off, and Heugen bowed his farewells to the Hopeforger cleric, his rival in the Red House, and last of all to W'starrah, who turned to extend her hand. I watched to see if Heugen, like all the other men I knew, was affected by her presence—with these nobles, it's really hard to tell. Mias was certainly letting his feelings be known, even I spotted it—looking at Hammer's flinty, focused demeanor, I wasn't sure whether he counted as a man.

Heugen left, taking all assurance of a predetermined vote for the Overlord with him. The city nobles would follow his lead, if he gave one, along with several guilds particularly indebted to his Color—Mias could probably calculate which those were, and his face told me he didn't like the odds. W'starrah still looked out the window, perhaps to hide her face, and I could tell with her guard half-down that now she was a bit disappointed. Did she hope for Huegen's vote, or his love? Or was there even more to this? From fifty paces away and without her gaze on me, I felt as if I was on fire—it was much more than lust, in fact the thought of making love to such a woman was intimidating. But the Stargazer priestess leveled you, made you feel like only one man among the milling throng, while you thirsted to be unique. Worthy of her attention, her conversation, perhaps even to impress her. As I looked on her, it seemed my gaze was actually filming over, maybe in the sheer brightness of a presence unlike any other.

46

I realized then that my senses had been trying to tell me something, while I crouched drooling. Not the priestess—or not just her. I didn't imagine smoke. I smelled it.

The bell-tower rang out above me and I almost fell off the roof from the shock. As I ran to find a back-way down to the ground, I could feel heat beneath my soles, and now the smoke was drifting up more thickly. The council chamber would be partly cut off; I could picture the main hall beneath me stuffed with flames. As I started to lower myself, my mind was already carrying the body where it would go next; a small postern behind the main apse, opening into a cherry orchard under the far stairway, that would be the only escape. Coming down took forever, and now the guards were shouting for priests first, water second. I hit the ground with my feet moving and doubted I would be the only one there when I arrived.

Argens' legend is rife with fire—the hero who held a slice of the sun in his hands inspired followers who treated it with respect. As absurd as it sounded, there would have to be rites observed, chants made, before anyone could fight the fire in their own temple. The attackers must have known that—and I didn't spare a moment's thought for the idea of an accident. I forced myself to walk and rounded the corner in sight of the postern while hugging the church wall shadow. The door was still closed, and I feared the worst; but when it suddenly kicked open I watched the boles of the nearby trees; two of the trunks grew wider, then split. I circled away from the wall and behind them.

From the door emerged three forms, two females and the enormous bodyguard, wreathed in smoke and half-doubled from coughing. The Nubian, hefting his massive spear, shook his head before lurching past the next corner to spy the way on. Behind him, the women crouched and coughed and leaned on each other; flickering red light from within the church shone on W'starrah's gown, and the other woman, still wearing her cloak, seemed frail and small next to her display. Perhaps twenty paces to one side of them, the two forms closed silently in unseen; another twenty paces back, I gave chase. But I was going to be too late.

"Milady," gasped the cloaked one, "where should we—"

"Stay with me, Kat," the priestess managed, patting her. "Chaktha will return as soon as he's seen where we are."

While one of the two attackers closed in with a small mace in hand, his companion paused to heft a dagger. Mistake—you shouldn't throw unless you're desperate. But he would have hit the priestess, if she hadn't bent over to cough again. It snapped into the stone behind the women and they looked up to perceive their danger. The other had closed the distance and raised the mace high. Which made me desperate. I kept running and side-flicked one of my throwing stars. It nicked the elbow and produced a yelp of pain; the blow came down glancing across the other woman's head, felling her like a scarecrow off a broken pole. W'starrah shouted—not screamed—for her guard and stepped over her companion's body. The closer assailant, recognizing the danger, stuffed a free hand over her mouth before she could incant; his partner closed in with another knife drawn for a thrust. At a run I barreled into the entire group of them, and we fell like a clot of wrestling children.

I smelled something beneath the cloud of jasmine the priestess wore, but now was definitely not the time. I rolled to my feet with one assassin clutching my leg, and overbalanced slamming my shoulder blades against the wall. One point of pain not caused by Simith, at least. Noises were rising from all over the temple grounds, and the world was starting to get light from the fires licking out the many upper windows. I scrabbled for my *noun-chakas* as the other raised his mace and turned to W'starrah, who lay still on her stomach, stunned by the impact. I didn't have time to get the hafts whirling, and settled for blocking with both in one hand as the attacker struck down on his target. The mace was small and the wielder very quick, forcing me away. His partner, getting to his feet, took one lick at me with the dagger, which I twisted to avoid, and then spun on the priestess.

The other woman had gotten to her hands and knees and saw it coming. She flung her body without hesitation over W'starrah's, and the assailant hesitated. My foe, pressing the attack, suddenly sprouted a shaft the size of a fencepost from the torso, gurgled and went down. I lunged at the dagger-wielder and again tackled two people to the ground. This time the other woman was the unlucky one on the bottom, and I heard her head strike the pavement, where it bounced and she lay still. Behind me I heard a basso voice bark "Priestess!" and from the corner of my eye saw Chaktha leap in, having followed the spear to defend his mistress. Without sparing a glance for the melee, the giant black scooped up the priestess the way I would grab a book, placed her over one shoulder and jogged back around the corner towards the entrance to the temple grounds. I heard her broken curses and protests as she dangled there.

I was up and the *noun-chakas* whirled; my foe was dazed and unsure, deprived of the target. But I give credit, there was no hesitation. Holding up a surprisingly feminine arm, the attacker calmly sliced one wrist, stepped back and dropped the knife. A breath later, the assassin fell to the stone; I knew the work of poison when I saw it.

I had only moments now to figure out what really happened here. The Lavender Lady was safe, out in the light and among the crowds, plus protected by that great bear of a guard. Who wanted her killed—I hated to suspect the answer already. Only three persons besides W'starrah even knew she would be here tonight—and I felt pretty sure that Z'kammet Hammer wouldn't gain much of an edge over a rival temple by setting his own on fire. From up the stairway I heard his distant bellow for someone to get out, and then Mias' voice in reply, screeching that the carpet was one of *his*.

I stepped over the poor woman to roll the assassin on her back. A female, sure enough, with a face pinched by more than just pain—I quickly checked her staring eyes and saw signs, even in death, as well as that drawn-in look to the neck, the wrists and at the waist. Lith was always deadly if you took it enough. And sooner or later you took enough: the poison had not cut off many days from this life. No wonder she was so fast. Searching for any identifying sign, I stripped off the gloves, opened the neck, and jerked up the black tunic at the waist. On the belt shone a steel buckle of simple but elegant workmanship, a shade of azure-blue so strong it practically shed its own light. Of course—the Grip had left before the fire, hadn't he?

The other woman stirred and groaned and I turned to look her over even as the guards started to pound down the stairs shouting incoherently. I saw a wisp of solid silver hair covering the woman's face, and stood back a bit towards the wall as her hand rose to clear it. Her arm under the cloak was draped with red, and a white border.

A shock ran through me as if I had been scratched by the deadly dagger at my feet. Ekatarinye, that had been her name. My teacher, the one who had opened the door of the world to me and whose youthful beauty drew my first hopeless love. Elves do not know, until their aging stops, at what time of life they will spend the centuries. The woman was still undeniably lovely, her small frame and delicate features improved in some ways by age. But she was no longer the image of a Stargazer priestess. I wondered if her wisdom helped her to face the centuries ahead as an elder in shape as well as soul. She lay back still stunned but would soon arise. I knew she was safe for now as well. Stooping, I carefully took up the dagger and cut loose both the assassins' belt buckles. Dropping the knife I stuffed my prize in a holster and dove away into the night.

Looking back from the outer wall, I could see the fire was well under control; the temple was festooned with hangings and rugs, but the bones were solid rock and money would fix the rest. I grinned to think tomorrow night's coronation parties might have to be displaced. Maybe after all, the Stargazers... but there were simpler explanations at hand. My warehouse hideout was not far and I could hole up there and think for the rest of the night. As adventurous an evening as Feldspar had spent, something in me wasn't ready for the challenge of being Jonn Simith again so soon. I might even sleep, a bit, after a day like this one.

$$\oplus \; \oplus \; \oplus$$

I truly did sleep, well past noon and awoke with aches in every joint. I was back in my normal quarters, in the abandoned warehouse from the south-eastern precinct, and it was quiet even in mid-afternoon. I rolled off my bunk, lit a candle, chewed some jerky and started to limber up.

Through the ceiling of my subterranean room I came into the warehouse behind a cove of heavy crates that looked solid from across the way. Checking around briefly, I confirmed that I was alone here, as always during the daytime. The last guild to make a delivery to this warehouse was when the Emperor Viridian was still alive. I tackled the climbing ropes first, ascending and descending with just the arms, then just the knees, and finally going into gentle swings and catches across the lattice of lines that webbed the roof level shadows. The sweat worked up nicely, and I could feel my heart and breathing under control as I kipped and swung in a zig-zag, varying my routine with sudden decisions. Twice I released and arced down to a pile of crates, tumbling, leaping and catching another rope to preserve my momentum as quickly as I could. My scrapes and bruises faded to nothing—the delight of the risk dissolved my earthly pain as it always did.

I stopped and sat atop a high pile of boxes, forcing my lungs to catch breath in a measured, near-silent way and looking down on my little kingdom. The warehouse had been my home, more than any other place since my time in the theater. Unknown to my fellow actors, I actually lived there in those days—circling back after the lock-up to sleep on the stage or under a balcony. During the day, no one ever came to the warehouse, and I could relax—no make-up, no need to hide who I was. Or ask.

As my breathing calmed I started to feel restless, as if I needed to be doing something else, or going somewhere else. From atop the crate pile I began to think about the previous night, when last I had been this high off the ground. W'starrah Altieri had accepted the invitation of her rival from the Hopeforger sect to meet and decide the new Mark. No question, there was enough power in the room to do that—no question, it was Hammer who held the balance, or else the meeting would have been elsewhere. Yet he invited her, out of a loose group of several, to represent the Stargazers; I was sure that Hammer, of all men in the city, wasn't just hoping for another view. So that meant her star was on the rise.

And the Red House was ready to assist, which was another coup; I didn't expect the Hopeforgers to be cozy with Carnad Mias. But then, perhaps that was what Altieri brought to the table, a lover with clout. He certainly wanted that, why should he be different? But it all fell down when the Fire Grip bowed out, so proper as always. And it made simple sense to me that Gaspar Heugen would be unwilling, to join people he was trying to incinerate.

I didn't care one way or another, politics was only the backdrop that created commissions for me. But something nagged—that attack was so... crude. No, that wasn't it—dead was dead. A fire would certainly seem accidental with all the blazing lights the Hopeforgers insisted on; and the attackers lurked in the orchard to make double sure it would succeed. Wait, now… how did they get in, and did those two set the fire or was there—wait again! I realized with a flash there was a more important question. The way my second attacker was willing to die, rather than retreat. I had seen fanatical devotion before, yet these could not have been either Hopeforgers or Stargazers, based on the targets. Neither sect countenanced suicide anyway.

It started to come to me now, and the hot flush of shame came with it—what was making me so dense these days? Poison, the use of lith, suicidal willingness—those two were ex-Vipers. The secret enforcers of the previous regime, outlawed by Yula now and all dead, or so the authorities would cheerfully assure us. Someone found a few, and suborned or tempted them (all it needed was the drug, with that second one)—that was what I had smelled in the melee, but was too confused to recognize. No, something else, a smell like… the sea? Damn my own hide, I couldn't think.

I started throwing stars around the upper level, not caring much about my aim but trying to bury each one deeper and deeper in the wood. I was beyond annoyance now, slipping into anger, and I couldn't tell why. More training—I lifted and angled, flipped and ran until I was seeing sparks. That suited my mood. What was the problem? Of course, I didn't know what was going on with my commission, but that was only to be expected—ignorance of the full terms was sauce on the meat for Feldspar. I would find out eventually. But I was—discontent. I looked around the warehouse, and the buzzing only got worse. The thoughts finally broke in on me unbidden, and only then did I realize I'd been holding back. On the memory. I started to laugh. My time among the undead.

The memories came flooding back like it was yesterday—not so odd, really, since it had been last week. The group of guardsmen who came in nights to drink, gamble and laugh were an annoying intrusion. No chance they could find my secret room—not that they even looked—and my kit up in the rafters went unnoticed. But my place had been invaded; I was determined to get them gone. Some method that kept the louts outside, and didn't alert the world to the presence of the most famous stealthic in the city. In hindsight, I could think of seven ways—how about a new lock on the door? I barked a murderous laugh at myself and kicked over a crate of musty cloth-bolts. No, no, I had to rise above such simple and effective solutions. Feldspar needed to address this problem with panache, with style, with genius.

So I had become a ghost.

There was a production at the theater a decade ago, a play about a time Overlord Toll'k'r was in trouble—rebellion against the Empire, probably—and consorted with one of those pagan preachers of the Bedou-uu. The foreigner claimed he could summon the ghost of Toll'k'r's father, and of course the Overlord decided there was nothing wrong with that. I knew from the start the spirit's role was mine—the costume was so elaborate and none of the others liked wearing the mask, or being seen as evil. For me, the joy was all in the creation of the ghostly persona—the paste of sphalerite and silver ore painted onto the tunic, the harness to lift me just a few inches from the ground, and of course the marvelous bulls-eye lantern with the sheet of glass.

I walked over to a dusty corner and pulled off the covering tarp. It was all still there. I had refined it since those days when the audience screamed in terror—some fled insisting the place was haunted, and that memory had stayed with me. People can't believe that large empty spaces are uninhabited. And I *knew* my plan would work.

It did, too well. On the chosen night I spent hours getting everything positioned and moved several stacks of crates to make a blind wall towards the back of the warehouse. The sight-lines were clear from above the crate-pile to where the men always sat to drink and roll the dice. On the ground level but completely blocked by mounds and rows of crates, I set the lantern and dangled before it about ten steps away. The glass plate, slanted overhead larger than a door and polished like a mirror, picked up my glowing reflection when I stepped on the pedal that opened the bulls-eye. I had added a warped lens of thick, uneven glass to the lantern, so that through the plate, seemingly floating a foot above the highest crate, a strange and shifting, semi-human shape appeared.

I could not even start the speech I had prepared before the men bolted screaming like children. They broke the hinges clean off the door and I could hear their shrieks for a minute afterwards. I laughed until the tears came and then went to bed, satisfied I had earned another ovation from the world's most critical audience, myself. The genius of Feldspar, and the ruin of my scheme as surely as the lead character of any tragedy I'd ever undertaken. Just like them, I'd seen nothing wrong until the end.

I kept the machine in place in case anyone tried to come back, and a week later they did. I dressed and prepared with a spring in my step, knowing their previous terror would only work in my favor now. Once more I took my position, settled my mask into place, and stepped on the pedal.

How was I to know they would bring a cleric with them!

Smiling ruefully, I re-covered the equipment and paced into the main chamber of the warehouse with my hands behind my back. The preachers of Cryssigens perform wondrous miracles, assuredly; making light in the darkness and fire from nothing, that was common. When the Hopeforgers cast a blessing, people always *felt* better; could the Stargazers really entrance the will, or were people just happy to help? But laying the undead—I had never heard of such a thing. No one had, while Viridian ruled and the reverence of Telhol was banned. Healing, that was all I had heard about them—of course, that wouldn't get anyone outlawed. I hung there in the harness that night, already in my pose and ready to speak when I heard one of them yell, "There, holy father, banish him!"

I froze, unsure as when a fellow actor gives the wrong cue, and then heard a male voice, not loud but very, very steady and sure, intoning words in the ancient tongue. He wasn't lying, that I knew for certain. I felt a chill run through me as never before in my life. I was caught, utterly foiled. The new emperor had freed Telhol's preachers from their underground existence, and these idiots had run off and found one, somewhere. I could tell from his tone that he believed his miracle effective—if I defied it, I would be immediately exposed. I had to be destroyed.

I admit it was one of my better performances. I twisted back and forth on my ropes as if in pain, uttering the most awful shrieks I could devise. Above me I could see my reflection bending and shivering. Heaving myself against the ropes at my back I kicked up hard into the sheet of glass, caterwauling in agony as it shattered along with my image. Then silence, not even a breath as I swung there and waited. The guards, who had been screaming too, started to exclaim for joy, praising Telhol and clapping the cleric on the back. I never heard his voice again, but I peeked between the crates and saw him; thin, short, light brown beard, an uncle's face, not a ghost-slayer. They left me to myself that evening as they practically carried him off to a tavern, though he shook his head smiling. I had hours to clean up, go back downstairs and think.

And what I came up with, a few days later, was a normal life. Now I looked around and realized I was homesick, standing in the middle of my own home. Suddenly I felt an urge to dress down and go back to Simith's house. Just as suddenly, I determined that would be the last thing I'd do tonight. I cleaned up, picked the bravo and got in disguise. I had always loved this outfit—the added nose was quite attractive, and the bright variety of colors across the cape, doublet and sash left everyone guessing about my House. But in the mirror it seemed somehow old.

It was too early, and the inn I chose felt tasteless. Everyone was buzzing about tomorrow's ceremony, and I could not scrape up one iota of interest. The ale had no savor, and there was no bard. Walking the streets, I returned the arrogant glances of the other sword-bearers and actually thought about picking a fight, just for something to do. I suddenly found my steps taking me closer to the Tepid, to The Boards. Angrily I turned around and almost ran back to the warehouse as full night set in. I had to hurry as I packed up my Feldspar garb and kit—the guards were daytime workers and could be here any moment. Rushed out of my own home! I was furious—and when a sudden thought suggested I had another home, I almost shouted with rage and denial.

What was the matter with me? I stormed back to the Stargazer temple, still dressed as the bravo, with every intention of collecting my commission. I would attend sunset service, do a little more scouting, and then find a secluded place to change.

But outside the main temple, W'starrah stood with another figure. I thought of Ekatarinye at once, and felt a pang of worry. But this was a young elf, slender and small, dressed in the drab grey of a day laborer. Once again I stopped outside hearing range; I recognized her mother in the girl's face and family is the only thing that interests me less than politics. This conversation, judging by the mother's importunity and the daughter's sullen refusal, might be both. The girl turned and left in mid-sentence—I bet that didn't happen to W'starrah Altieri very much. Something about the younger woman's poise was striking, she was determined but showed no sign of anger.

My attention, of course, was on the mother; she smiled after the plain-dressed girl, shook her head, and turned to enter the temple. I followed at a distance, but stopped when I saw her enormous bodyguard under the eaves, watching everyone who entered like a hungry raptor. I got a twinge of alarm—for a brief, confused moment last night, we had been within spitting distance. Rumor had it this giant black was born in the southern jungle, with the senses of the beasts he hunted there. It grated on me, but I never took chances for nothing. Getting caught here involved no risk for Hope, just an inconvenience. So the bravo made a brief show of indecision, then strode off the temple grounds as if he had remembered an urgent appointment.

I found a shaded alley and changed into my night clothes, then made my way by rooftop back to The Boards. I was defeated—no more progress tonight, and I could not stomach the thought of those guards spilling ale on the warehouse floor and telling jokes they had forgotten two days earlier. The neighborhood was quiet, and I slipped into my second story window after prizing the latch. As soon as I set the pane back in place I felt trapped, as if in jail. In a fit of deliberate pique I did not change into Simith's clothes. Maybe if I broke another chair, I'd feel better.

Too restless to sleep, I unpacked the crate and set the tools aside, then started working on the house. I quietly cut a roof-hatch in the upstairs lavatory, as well as a pivoting escape-panel in my bedroom behind the headboard where the joints would not show. Getting in and out unseen was the first priority: time enough for bolts and traps later. Who would ever want a non-entity like Jonn Simith dead—then I remembered the mugging and chuckled grimly.

The kitchen was completely stocked, and fortunately some of the food was fruit. On the counter lay one gold, three silver pieces and seven bits. I left them there for now—my attitude towards coins was unchanged and I had enough headaches already. Maybe I could sleep. Maybe tomorrow would be better. Maybe I could get back into my own skin before it killed me.

⊕ ⊕ ⊕

J kept dreaming someone was pounding at my door and I needed to escape. But the house had become enormous, with three extra floors, crossing halls, and privies everywhere. Each room I entered had a secret hatch cut into it, but they were all spiked from the outside. I finally found my master bedroom at the end of a long hall, and I knew, the way the dreamer always knows, that the panel behind my headboard would work. The room was crammed with chairs from wall to wall, but I managed to wrestle my way past them as the pounding got louder and louder. I pushed on the panel and fell through into the warehouse floor. An arm tugged me up and I saw the face of a kindly uncle in preacher's robes, who said "It's over." Just as I realized his hand on my arm was too small, I woke up.

I had fallen asleep on the kitchen counter, half a tangerine still clutched in one hand. On a level with my face was Keilee's; the kitchen door was slightly open and she was shouting at me with urgency. I had never felt so groggy, hazed with confusion and my body a mass of aches.

"Mister Simith! What are you doing here, the morning's over! You need to HURRY!"

I shook my head and looked over at the urchin—she did have rather large eyes, perhaps that was the reason I had such trouble talking to her. "Easy, little one, easy, is your, ahm, home on fire?"

She rolled her eyes and kept tugging until I swung down and got my legs under me. Everything below my waist tingled with the violent shock of cut-off blood; I nearly buckled to the floor. "No, silly," she practically shouted, "the arena, you have to hurry! Get dressed and go!"

With a shock I realized I had not changed into Simith's clothes. Looking down, I saw I had stripped off most of Feldspar's outfit while working on the hatches. Only the black pants were left, looking too tight but suitably smudged with sawdust and not standing out much. My naked chest—and its scars and bruises—evidently gave Keilee no concern, as she practically slapped me towards the stairs and my room. "Hurry! Everyone in the city will be there, all the grown-ups, and you're going to miss it! The new Overlord, today, hurry!" I could hear the jealousy in her voice, and felt a little charge of her enthusiasm. Normally I hated anything to do with ceremony, but today promised to be quite a show. I might pick up a few clues to my commission from W'starrah's actions. And I had missed the arena since the new emperor's ban.

"As you wish, mistress," I said with affected gentility, "I shall get myself dressed and make my way to the center of town. And I shall be certain to give you all the details when I return," I added as I started up the stairs.

"Good, you had better." Keilee was a practical girl; she needed me for a source of information. But as I headed up I heard steps on the tread behind me and realized she intended to follow. Enough was enough—I had to put a stop to this.

"I know I show little evidence, but I do have the ability to dress myself, madam."

Her face fell a bit, and I got another shock to see her standing in my foyer. "Just how, exactly, did you, ahm, get in?"

She shrugged. "I pounded and kicked on your front door. I threw rocks at the bedroom window—at the shutters. Finally I went around to the side." My heart fell as I realized—last night when I left as Feldspar I had not locked the door behind me! Idiot, moron, amateur—the entrance to my hideout in the warehouse was concealed, but had never been locked.

"Well and good, madam," I said a bit tersely, "but you will find I can manage today, thank you."

"I came by to make your dinner last night, after I delivered the groceries."

"Yes, I was out late," I said, "not to worry. And do not bother this evening either, I shall manage." I saw the pain in her face then; nice work, elegantly done. Good thing there were no chairs to break on the stairs. But I was too rushed to think about it, so when she turned to leave I bounded up to the bedroom and grabbed my Simith garb. I locked both doors on the way out, and Keilee was nowhere to be seen in the neighborhood. I knew she would recover at the next interesting thing to happen.

If I had no idea what was happening today, I would still have known where to go. The city was flowing in the same direction, a human river with a current of excitement. Within a few blocks I was getting crowded in—again, my whole face tingled as it would whenever there was something to protect. But today it was just me—after awhile I felt oddly free. I smiled companionably at Giurid across the way with Delith, and they waved with a score of bodies between us. Up ahead I saw the barrelmaker looming over most others, with a woman I presumed his wife on one arm, creating a little wake where I could walk in comfort. Children zipped between the smallest, temporary spaces in the flow of flesh, screaming and tagging and begging adults they had never seen before for permission to attend. But every adult knew better, though it humored some as it angered others to be so pestered.

I sluiced onto Altair Way with hundreds of my fellow-citizens, into a carnival atmosphere. Which, in Cryssigens, meant just another day. Six dawns a week, and the saying goes "two centuries-old festivals, two parties invented last week, and for the rest—a little rest!" Some had draped the streetside windows at the center of the city, and the House colors were in full evidence; folks even of modest means dressed from head to toe in orange, blue, or yellow, a living sign of their allegiance that would no doubt gain them a better seat. Now the river clogged more frequently as the noble retinues passed by ahead of the crowd. When they were too far ahead to see, tempers got short as folks pressed to continue and couldn't see the reason for the delay. But a nearby passing was a pageant inside a parade. Litters, horses, musicians, banners, all were standard. I saw the basket-weavers guild go by with a boy atop a camel, lobbing little reed birds into the crowd that fluttered and glided to the hands of delighted children on all sides. I caught one to examine, as all working things interest me. A nice gesture—and they had two attendants to sweep up behind the camel, even better.

Then the final crush as we neared the gates; the press of flesh became threatening to everyone, not just those with secrets to keep. I insinuated myself smoothly through the gaps until I was directly behind Staveshaver, the barrel-maker. He was able to shield me somewhat from the inevitable push-backs that happened as the guards jostled the eager masses. After a few moments it gained an air of hilarity, driven by our common eagerness and good spirits; some group of worthies far behind us started to yell "Heave!" in concert, and I was literally taken off the ground as the tide pushed forward with chuckles and a few screams of protest, then away as the guards ordered and barred and shoved back. Droke Staveshaver in front of me was not amused, and more than held his own, which left me more room to chuckle about it. With each lap of the human tide we came a bit closer to the gates, and finally I was through and into the arena.

I took in the filling stands, the brilliant sunshine and the sound of horns and drums on all sides. The arena worked its magic on me, even after more than two hundred days away. We entered in a mingled wave of shade and station, but the people sorted themselves out as they sought their seats. On the side of honor, near the empty throne of the Overlord, a small section of privileged seats for the ranking nobles was flanked on all sides by the great swathes of Blue and Red, the two ranking Houses of Cryssigens. Across the arena, beyond the central table where the leaders would vote, the Yellow took the center spot, and the second-rank Colors in smaller stripes arrayed themselves to its wings. I never realized before how small the Purple House was; its fame and influence was largely due to its rarity, which kings and emperors wore, as well as the remarkable recent career of the Lavender Lady.

Guilds for iron-mongering, sailing, pottery and more filled in the next-best seats; usually I dressed as Chay, Simith's fictional employer, and sat with the masons when I attended the gladiatorial games. But today I was content to drift along towards the end of the stadium where the people of my new precinct were settling in. Some of the tavern crowd called me over, holding a seat and I laughed aloud with them at the comradery and good feeling. The festive mood was buoyant, as everyone expected a quick vote and a long celebration to take the holiday well into the night. I had my doubts, seeing what I had; still, the mood was unbreakable.

Trumpets blared and the city's elite entered one by one to take their seats at the table. I saw Hammer walking stiff as a rod and looking just as disappointed as when Heugen left his chambers. W'starrah made an enormous splash with the litter and her gown, even from a

60

furlong away a dazzling jewel set appropriately between Mias in his red and the blue sash of the Fire Grip Heugen. Other preachers and guild-masters, two of the three barons and several knights took their seats as well, until the empty chair for the Emperor's designate loomed by comparison on the end closest to me. I recalled the knowing sailor from the Grog's Lees and wondered about the audacity of anyone who would order an assault on imperial troops. Maybe I needed to seek someone who also had the guts to set fire to the largest church in Cryssigens. But why would one do the other? It was all beyond me.

I watched W'starrah. She seemed pleased as a cuddled kitten at the ovation for her appearance, but when she sat for the invocation I saw something tenser, less self-satisfied. She had no assurances from her conclave, and feared losing the vote. But who would it be? Even I felt some excitement now.

Yet my interest drowned completely, when the screeching nightmare fell from the sky almost on top of the table itself. Everyone around me screamed and fell between the benches to cower; I certainly flinched and shrank back, but managed to keep my eyes working though my ears were deafened in the panic. The beast looked like a cart-sized eagle grafted to a skiff-length lion, neither one being happy with the result. It landed heavily with a thunderous concussion I felt through the stands below. At once, it churned the hard-packed arena earth like a flower-bed. I marveled at the unbroken fury of it, much better than any of the creatures I had seen in this arena in all my years. Its wings spread wider than the table and the beak looked sharp enough to bite a man in half. When I saw a human figure on its back, at first I refused to believe it. He wore the uniform of an imperial officer and held a sun-decked flag. I had never spared any time to do more than hate the empire and its soldiers, like any good citizen. Yet it was clear to me, whatever else, this one understood risk. My respect rose a notch.

Everyone at the main table had fallen back or beneath it for protection, except for Gaspar Heugen, who stood with one hand on his weapon. On the other side, a lone preacher also kept his seat and offered no resistance. The rest, even W'starrah had all shrunk down; only a bit faster than the audience who would shortly see them, did they regain their feet or chairs. The imperial soldier dismounted and advanced on the table after planting his flag in the arena dirt. He radiated confidence, and when his monstrous mount screamed again—making everyone around me dive back for cover—he turned about and slapped it with his crop. Not an ounce of fear in that one—I saw the face of a soldier it would be very, very bad luck to have as an enemy.

Of course, he might not have talked so tough without that barn-sized beast behind him. I could see the table bristling from hostility as the man cocked his chin high and announced there would be no voting today. People all around me shouted with disappointment, and I thought for a moment I'd have a mob to duck. But that monster screeched again and all our courage dissolved.

I watched W'starrah. Her face had actually relaxed and she smiled winningly at the newcomer speaking words of welcome. It was more than flirtation, she was glad there had been no vote and hadn't expected to avoid it. The haughty officer almost let his jaw fall open, then managed something in return. I saw one of the local knights challenge him with a question, and the emperor's officer turned to answer him sharply. Our man was decked out in silver and red, not a hair out of place and years of noble training behind him. The newcomer was scuffed and rumpled, his uniform nearly as worn as his flag. But across the table from this warrior, our knight looked like a children's toy in a store: he sat down furious but without another word.

Our religious leader Z'kammet Hammer announced a delay, two months, before a return to voting, and the high and mighty tried their best to huff off the arena stage without giving their backs to that thing. I turned to go with the others, but stopped at the exit to take another look at the emperor's man who stayed behind. He stood there like a statue, completely alone in the center of the arena, looking very hard but small in the shadow of the beast he had ridden to town. Captain Justin, people around me muttered; claimed he had a company of men marching north to join him by tomorrow. Things were only getting more interesting.

No need for the taverns today—everyone had seen the same thing and speculation wouldn't bring me any closer to the truth. While most of the city decided to celebrate despite the lack of an occasion, I fretted the afternoon away back at the warehouse. I donned my working clothes hours early and practically shouted with impatience for the sun to go down. Back to the Stargazer temple; I couldn't wait any more, Feldspar wanted to work and he wanted to know.

But it was hurry up to wait, as things turned out. No service that evening, no big celebration either. The temple buzzed with folks fluttering back and forth asking their superiors what, if anything, to do. The superiors sent messengers asking each other the same thing. I could see important guild leaders and even some House Color embassies asking for consultations with their Stargazer allies. Both moons were up in the early evening tonight, which made things a bit trickier as I moved across the temple grounds. Still I felt practically among friends here; any arrester would take me straight to the priestess anyway. It was a matter of pride—I wanted to slip in and out unseen, better for my reputation since my employers invariably wanted my commissions kept secret.

W'starrah's chambers were ablaze with lanterns, though most callers were being turned away from the entrance to her tower. Two guards in red silks, clearly marking time, stood by while Chaktha loomed at the entrance. So, the Cup of Red again. From the gazebo, I could make out lantern light and soft talk from the left-hand chamber. Whatever she was saying to Mias was covered by the nonstop carping of his two guards; their litany of a difficult life drew only monosyllables from the Nubian.

I resolved to use the right-hand window, and be in milady's private quarters when she finished with her company. Until then, I grasped some of the flowering vines on the gazebo sides, yellow and blue blossoms that smelled of a clean shore, and my hands remembered the weave we were taught as schoolchildren. A love-knot, I forgot the symbolism, but to use the blue and yellow meant admiration for the recipient. I smiled a thought of Ekatarinye, who taught us how to send these messages, many thoughts signaled by color, type of bloom, shape, size. There was always a layer beneath the surface, a meaning disguised by appearances—no doubt she knew that now.

The minutes stretched on; once when the guards paused, trying to think of something else to natter about, I caught a whiff of the conversation above me.

"This bears further... examination," Mias said with a hint of innuendo.

"I shall honor the silversteel token, milord," W'starrah responded in a complex alto. If the Red House Cup had brought a token to the temple, it meant an obligation to spend the evening. Whether they made love was not the point: with priestesses of the highest level, most men didn't dare. But the assignation itself was a mark of honor Carnad Mias could boast of the rest of his blubber-ribbed life. How could he have come by a token? A silver one, certainly, and that seemed more suited to his tastes. My heart sank, not just from the wait, not simply from the wave of jealousy that this fat carker was there, but from some other instinct that remained beyond words. Him, here with her was—wrong.

My hands continued their work, better than I had expected when I started out. I don't recall deciding, but before the weaving was half-done I resolved to leave it for my former teacher. Not love, exactly, not anymore, and I knew it was wrong to do so anonymously. But I never doubted she would still be the children's tutor, and when I was done I slipped down and stole to the schoolhouse. I spotted a rare lotus floating in the pool nearby, red tinged with white, and plucked it for the center of the knot, to leave no doubt. I left it wedged in the classroom door and moved back to the tower, shaking my head and chuckling a bit.

Returning from one side of the curving wall, I was surprised to hear the outer door open and Mias' voice instructing his guards to follow. Now I tasted disgust—a quick toss, for the highest ranking female among the Stargazers? Was the man mad? I hugged the wall out of their view and began to climb when the moons were right. The carvings of Argens' many wives were amply curvaceous, and I had no trouble waiting for the shadows cast by quick-moving Aral to pass. But it took me several minutes to stay out of sight.

Angling toward the right-hand window, I heard W'starrah talking and assumed it was to one of her attendants. I was at the sill and about to climb across when I heard a male voice answer her briefly, and I froze as if in combat. I could not make out all the words, but it was definitely not the tone of a menial.

"My life," he said, "is the least thing I would lose for the prize I seek."

"Wait here," W'starrah said urgently, "I will bring you what you need."

I ducked below the sill as she breezed into the inner chamber and opened a small casket by the bedside. It seemed she did something with her hands, but when she turned back none of her jewelry seemed changed. Back in the outer room, she addressed her visitor with a more confident tone, as if she had established control of something.

"To the north then," she said, "and the power you can bring back from there."

"To the north, milady," the man responded with quiet purpose. When his boots stepped towards the outer door I used the time to slip inside and take up a perch atop the highest dresser in a corner, visible to the one lowered lantern across the room but draped in shadow. Was W'starrah hiring agents left and right? Who was this fellow? I only heard him speak a few words but they carried such determination. Then I thought of the assassins and my blood froze.

No more time to speculate; she came back in, deep in thought and I took a moment to gird myself mentally for the burden of her attention. She drifted back to the jewelry box, and I watched her take off the plainest ring I had ever seen. The rest of W'starrah Altieri, of course, was perfect. Even from here, I took in the scent of jasmine; I noted the incense brazier in one corner and bet myself that the two smells were meant to mingle for a designed effect. She was holding her arms crossed beneath her splendid breasts as she thought, very gently and slowly swaying side to side. The piles of her lustrous champagne hair shifted across her shoulders when she changed the tilt of her head, clearly trying to decide something. She could break into a dance any moment and it would look the most natural thing in the world—more, this small shifting motion seemed the start of a dance. I had never recalled my collar feeling so tight before, and beneath the mask my face was returning heat enough to make my eyes blink. Best try to keep this appointment brief.

Before I could clear my throat to announce my presence, she stiffened and looked up. It startled her and I felt a small kick of energy, as if my end of the seesaw had gained a bit. I was up high as well, which also tended to give me an advantage. But after a quick look at the outer chamber in alarm, W'starrah gazed back up at me and gave a laugh with music in it; I felt the room start to tip down in her direction again.

"So! This is a busy evening, but I admit I bring it on myself. Do you, sirrah, have the token I'm told to expect?" This last was a mocking reference to my system, and I was glad she couldn't see my foolish grin as I thumbed out a piece of feldspar and held it to the light. She went back to her box, hesitated only a second—too late now, she must have thought—and turned back with the gem I had given to Tambouri Shai the other night. I held out my piece, and when she came underneath my perch I dropped it into her palm. She compared the numbers scratched on the back of each, a matching set. She nodded her approval.

"Welcome, Feldspar, I am delighted to meet you. Won't you join me down here?" With the ease born of long practice, she moved back to the bedside, swirled her long gown in a half-circle, took a goblet from the side-table and sat on a small stool set with a rounded pillow on top. It was a little lower than made for a comfortable seat, but considered in conjunction with the thick carpet beneath it… I scraped up enough sense not to move a muscle. I knew my mysterious appearance, bolstered by as little talk as possible, were the only advantages I had in this interview.

W'starrah waited a few moments more, then laughed again. "You must forgive me, noble sir—I really have no experience in hiring living legends." She twirled the cup gently between her palms with arms on knees, leaning forward only slightly, but enough to emphasize the divide of her chest and the elegant sculpture of her collar-bone where a necklace lay against the skin. She looked up suddenly and before I could glance elsewhere I took in the amber orbs, with such spirited intelligence I felt a charge run straight down to my knees. Here was the high priestess of those who foresaw the future, and I felt she could look through me like a pane of glass.

"What do you know, Feldspar, of the Brow of the Ecclesiast?"

While I desperately ransacked my brain for things Ekatarinye had patiently tried to teach those years ago, I gave a slight diagonal nod, the kind that says, "Of course, but you tell me."

"Created many centuries ago with the aid of northern craftsman as well as rustic lore, the Brow has always been worn by the highest ranking, most worthy of the preachers of the North Mark. Studded with gems of power worked into a braided circlet of mingled metals, the Brow bestows great power on the wearer. Power to inspire, to foresee… and to persuade." On this last, W'starrah's eyes came up again and locked with my own straight through the mask. And I saw—even as the charge ripped down through me again, I realized what the ambitious woman was about. Some of the history was coming back to me as she spoke. Risking my voice, I pitched it low and husky to say "Hammer."

"Yes!" she replied with vigor and eagerness. "Since the fall of the Demonbenders, the Hopeforger sect is supreme in Cryssigens, and Hammer is the acknowledged leader of that church, unlike our coterie, which seeks consensus. When the new emperor was seated in Argens, he ordered the Demonbender cult disbanded and outlawed, its leaders subject to imprisonment and its wealth confiscated by the leading church near to each of its former temples."

She smiled like a cat as she rose and walked to the window away from me. I felt some relief that her gaze had shifted, followed by a wave of loneliness I had never expected. I was still sweating from the effort of facing her, but part of me wanted the scrutiny back. And I admitted that the line of her thighs, flashing skin through the center slit as she walked, was nearly the match of the front of her. Yet I began to realize, as she talked on, that perhaps no man would ever be W'starrah Altieri's true love. She spoke with steeped desire now, when she talked of the power of the Brow.

"And before today, I will be honest with you, master Stealthic, I hoped to hire you to steal me this crown. With it, I could move the great stubborn stone that blocks our country's path to peace! I could—well. I believe I am worthy to wear the Brow, what of that? And the legends tell of horrible punishments for the one who dons it without merit. I am content to face that risk."

"But today—did you hear, my sly and skillful companion, what transpired at the arena today?"

For my answer, I took the reed bird from my tunic-sash and let it flutter circling down to land on her bed. Flirting a bit with that touch—and it seemed to work as the lady broke into a peal of delighted laughter and clapped her hands.

"Bravo! Yes, a remarkable interruption was it not? A day of surprises—" she mused, gazing a moment to the outer chamber. How could she have made love to Carnad Mias and still look so matchless? "But did you note something else, perhaps missed by the many in all that excitement?"

I could think of nothing, and gave a small shrug to cue her. She clearly wanted to tell the tale anyway.

"He wore no crown!" she cried in triumph, and I knew she meant Z'kammet Hammer. "I met with that man, just last night, to… negotiate. And in his meeting chambers, I saw the box—no question, the tales tell of the casket in which the Brow is kept. But today, my dear stealthic, the Ides of the Dolphin when every citizen expected a new Overlord to be crowned—the patriarch of the Hoperforger church came to the table with a head as bare as my own. If he was not worthy—ah, but you must put it on to find out, and so he would have died."

"I no longer wish you to steal the Brow of the Ecclesiast from Z'kammet Hammer, Feldspar. Because he doesn't have it."

I sat back a bit on my haunches then, and despite my best effort I nodded. Her smile from by the window was radiant, and she leaned back a bit with hands on the stone behind her to emphasize the figure that needed no assistance. A gift, for me. I looked off into a corner as if thinking about the job, instead of silk and soft curving skin and the scent of incensed jasmine. It was very much time to leave.

"I offer you five thousand pieces of silver, Feldspar, not for the return of the Brow, but merely for the knowledge of where it lies." She was smart, this one—she might get what she wanted by another avenue, and I understood the desire to have options. "If you do this for me—", this in a tone of currying a favor, "and it further should happen that a… retrieval is necessary, I offer you a further twenty thousand silver pieces." Enough to buy a large merchant vessel, stock it, sink it for fun, and build two more. As if the priestess did not already have my undivided attention.

"And more, my clever stealthic, oh prized of Astor," she breathed and stepped towards me across the room. "If you do this great thing, whatever befalls the next wearer, it will be known that you were the one to bring this jewel back into the light from wherever it has been lost. The Brow of the Ecclesiast will be crucial to crowning the next Mark of the North—I have seen it in the stars." No silly love-talk there—the Stargazers were astrologers of the first order and did not make such statements lightly. W'starrah's eyes blazed like planets now, seeing nothing and everything at once.

There came an excited knock on the outer door of her chambers, and W'starrah sank back to earth with a sigh of amused frustration. She turned and left the room in a swirl of purple silk, and I seized my chance like a drowning man. I dove off the wardrobe, tumbling on the thick carpet and grabbed up the two feldspar gems from the side-table. Having thus signified that I accepted the commission, I ran to the window as the pounding continued on W'starrah's door. I heard just the edge of a cry, whether of joy or fear, and was through the window and making my way down on the moon-lee of the tower.

As I slithered through slices of darkness on my way back to The Boards, I wondered about the intentions of my newest employer. Even now my outfit was wet with perspiration from my interview, but my head came back to me enough to distrust anyone who could exercise such influence. Did W'starrah Altieri really believe she was worthy to wear the Brow of the Ecclesiast? What worthy cleric would interview assassins, or lie with a House Cup to gain power? But why would she order Vipers to attack herself, with no one nearby to fool? I only knew two things for certain, and neither one of them made me happy. I knew I would never have a real chance to enjoy the love of W'starrah Altieri, and I knew also that I didn't need twenty-five thousand silver pieces.

But there was risk in play, maybe lots of it. And the service of Hope too. I'd have done the job for three silver bits, as long as I could find someone else to hold them for me.

$$\oplus \oplus \oplus$$

Where the mouth of the Tepid feeds the Western Sea, the shoreline rises even further than usual, creating a promontory that overlooks the entire city. Up there I could see the Crystal Palace, where the descendants of Cryss Altair ruled for the first seven centuries of the empire, and lesser houses thereafter. The hundreds of glass panes set into its surface always, always catch the light whether of sun, moon or stars, and man-made reflections from below amplify the effect. Gaspar Heugen lives there now, but only in the forward tower nearest the gate, reserved for the Fire Grip. The main palace, as far as anyone knows, lies empty. And the dungeons below the palace, cut far down into the stone of the sea-cliff, are only a rumor. The whispers of a demon made of pure glass, held prisoner and holding the roots of the city like a spider in its web, never find a glimmer of support, and never die away. I always had my doubts. A demon locked in an inaccessible prison for centuries—what does he eat?

I crouched on a rooftop looking down into the sunken dell below the palace, where lay the softly-smoking ruins of the chapel to Argens Demonbender. This was my first stop on the path of finding the Brow—in truth, the only one I could think of. Once the most privileged of churches, it had been as much a locus of power as the palace next door. When Yula's rebellion stripped away the mask and revealed that the cult was supporting its demon emperor, first with the collusion of Overlord Kreel and later his son Kreelon, the nobility naturally shied away from their former association. In the month of Gryphon last year, as the usurper outlawed the cult entirely, the common people moved in, storming the church and physically smashing it to match the political fall from favor. I wasn't there and hadn't paid attention. But now I had to admit, the mob did its work well.

A tale as old as childhood; something's been lost, and the person you appeal to has the same answer, the same pose with arms akimbo and furrowed brow. "Well, where did you see it last?" I had W'starrah's ingenious assertion that despite the box, the Brow of the Ecclesiast was not in the possession of Z'kammet Hammer and the church of Argens Hopeforger. Dressed as the bravo I had canvassed a few of the inns and slipped my questions into the general pissing about the lack of an Overlord. Ah yes, the Brow—wonderful thing I hear. No, cannot recall ever seeing something like that on Hammer's head. Remarkable, isn't it, he should so modestly forbear to have it on such an auspicious day. Just shows you the character of that noble cleric, true.

Of course, in the kind of tavern where lights burn bright and cups are clean, no one wishes to admit they had ever been to the temple of the Demonbenders. But the ripe old beggar went to some places on the waterfront—hardly inns, more an accidental collision of streetcorner, table and rum-bottles—and learned more. Sure, the preachers of Argens Demonbender used to wear the Brow on state occasions, big sermons, rituals, that sort of thing. "The last prelate to head the church, funny you should ask," one said, "that tall elf, Tarsi, related to the house of Kreel, he was in charge there until summer. Killed at Tor Perite last summer, wasn't he? Or was it the Battle of Broken Chains, last spring? Any and all, here's the thing—he used to carry it around during services, holding it up and parading it. Never wore it though, I'll swear to that."

I looked over the ruins as I tried to time the guards pacing the quarantined grounds. The weeping beeches, so mal-formed and ancient with bulbous, twisted trunks, now lay chopped and prostrate to all sides. Cracks peppered the roof, portals of massive wood or iron lay hanging by one hinge; yet the dark marble bones of the place were intact. This had never been a friendly edifice. The soft lines of the Stargazer temple were inviting and delightful; the soaring height of the Hopeforger church induced awe and inspiration. But this muscular pile of stone, intended to portray strength and endurance, now looked like an intruder, wounded and hugging the ground. Perhaps it was hiding a weapon in the earth beneath it. Maybe it was saving strength, in case the mob came back, to lash out one more time.

I could see a rent in the dome large enough to get through, but wasn't sure what handholds I could find on the ceiling within. Best to try a ground-level entrance, so I needed a blind-spot between the turns, pauses and inattention of the guards. I watched nearly an hour but saw little to pick on in their routine; impressive, as they had probably been at this for months. I came to the ground, entered the line of trees ringing the compound, and circled at a distance seeking a better angle. Far off on the back side of the temple someone had cleared a space, and poured in part of a foundation. I could see a modest pile of building stone with a few tools there, and what appeared to be a shed for storage made of flatwood scraps, the kind work crews erect to keep mortar from the rain. On the south side the brush grew close to the low stone wall, and I hit upon the simple expedient of waiting there for a guard near the mid-point of his passage. Once he went beyond me, I would have nearly half a minute to negotiate the four-foot wall, get into the inner grounds, and lay flat five or six rods away before he came back. Black clothing against dark ground out of direct moonlight—child's play.

The guard went past and I stayed where I was. The moments ticked by, but I kept looking at the pillars, the cracked doorway of the temple on this side, the complete lack of windows. Slowly it dawned on me that I was frozen in place. The guard came back and I waited impatiently for him to return. He passed by again and when he was out of hearing, I pushed hard on my knees to force myself to stand. I stood there like an idiot for ten full counts, staring down at my feet and wondering what language I needed to order them to move. Then I dropped to the ground again. This was new. Evidently my body was afraid of this place.

I studied the edifice again by the clouded moonlight. My head slowly settled, and I took out from the level of my instinct the things I feared. This wasn't some impossibly-long vault, or guards ratcheting crossbows. The walls didn't look likely to fall in; no one would blow a trumpet if I tripped. I faced those dangers all the time—I thrived on them. But something about the Demonbenders... I had never felt any desire to reverence Argens in that way, myself. But you could always tell those who did. One extreme or the other—couldn't wait to grovel before their betters, or couldn't hold back from lording it over the grovelers. Argens the Demonbender brooked no excuses, held back no power, thought nothing beyond daring. The preacher who built this place—back in the age when men created entire buildings overnight—summoned demons to his altar. And there he broke their wills, forced them to do his bidding. This was the cult that countenanced bringing evil to heel. Or so they always told us.

I felt something still alive there. Like the trickling smoke, I sensed evidence of a formless menace. These guards, men who hated me as much as Beirill, were my friends compared to that. Still and all, I said deliberately to myself, it is risk. Its shape is new, but that is nothing. When the form of a challenge is known, it stops being risky. I don't know if I can do this thing. That makes it worth trying.

A bit of fire rallied inside me—maybe this is how the knights felt when entering a hopeless battle. I played one once onstage, he declaimed he had become fey, reckless of his life. The guard passed again, and I rose as smoothly as if I were heading out to a store. One too-large step over the low wall, and I was on the temple grounds. I hid behind a downed trunk, and when the guard passed back I crept to the closest door and slipped inside.

I had to take a minute to adjust, with only a few rents in the walls and ceiling to filter some starlight. The entire space was one enormous room up to the dome and out to the walls, though I sensed some small chambers against the opposite side. Everywhere I looked, I made out the shape of wrack and anger; the mob had broken rails, torn curtains, twisted candle-pillars, even smashed the prayer-benches, which surely had done nothing wrong. Benches are inoffensive things, unlike chairs.

The smell stopped me too. Rot, and singeing odor, and something more, something far away from the scent of jasmine and incense. There was more smoke in here—months later, I marveled—which the moon and stars through the cracks did very little to define. I discerned shades of black and little more. From the holster belt I extracted my small lantern, set with a bulls-eye and thinner than my three bundled fingers. I adjusted the side-flaps and lit the wick, producing a small circle of light casting a foot across less than a body-length before me. Vaguely, I saw the benches had been shaped in an off-centered web, with aisles converging towards the altar at the western end of the main space. I began to make my way there.

I almost fell into a broken hole on the marble floor, and after smothering a curse I wondered what the mob could have done to cause such damage. The earth beneath the stone, more than three feet down, looked as dark as pitch, and the smell was even stronger here. But I felt a need to hurry. Nearest to the altar were rows of open space, with divots carved in the floor marking where worshippers might sit, or perhaps lie prostrate. Behind the altar space the statue of Argens rose beyond the sight of my lantern, dark red porphyry with one foot and the edge of his sword trapping a three-legged monster beneath him, its spine curved in submission. I shook myself a bit and moved closer.

In front of the low altar was a solid gold conjuring circle set right into the stone. Someone had picked at it in enough places to figure it

73

no longer worked for protection, but I gave it a berth in passing. There was a fair amount of wealth secreted in various places all around—gems, gold and silver workings, and several months ago many of the cloth hangings would have been fine enough to sell. Several hundred people crowded through here in chaos, with a prime opportunity for perfect crimes—who would rise to the defence of an outlawed cult? To have left so much behind, ruining but not taking, spoke to me of the same deep reluctance I was feeling now. The altar was empty and the lectern next to it contained only a book for services. I scanned around briefly before moving to the small chambers opposite, where I hoped the libraries were still intact.

Something caught the corner of my eye, up on the ceiling I thought. I froze and waited, watching, but nothing moved and it was far beyond my light's range. Normally my instincts for threat were excellent, but at last I decided it must have been a coil of smoke. The chambers were small wooden structures set against the far wall, little more than booths offering privacy. In the center of the row sat a low set of shelves with glass-front cases locking away the tomes. No one had so much as broken the glass, and I wasn't going to be the first. The locks were good, but hardly professional. I resheathed the pick and opened the first one to scan the titles.

I examined tomes at random, looking for something either very old or very recent. The order of the books, if there was one, escaped me; rituals of service mingled with historical logs of the temple's history as well as accounts of great leaders in past centuries. Some of the smaller books were written in a script I could not read—probably not Ancient, I could at least recognize that—and some of their pages were inscribed with pentagrams and other figures. Seemed a safe bet that nothing good would come of studying them, so I focused on the larger tomes.

Time slipped by and certain clues emerged. I spotted a brief reference to the creation of the Brow, from the middle of the seventh century ADR. The head of the church—evidently still a single church, but already arguing—was Mart'l'n Ecclese. He combined his own lore with that of a northern dwarf and a "shaman"—unfamiliar word, I guessed a leader of the pagan Bedou-uu. My jaw dropped open when I saw the dwarf was paid with a cubic foot of silversteel. The shaman, evidently, had some other item of jewelry created and took it back to the desert with him. Mart'l'n wore the Brow and was able to unite all the squabbling preachers of the Mark, so that the Overlord declared him Highforge, evidently in honor of his new headpiece.

So that was where Hammer's title came from. But if W'starrah was right, he hadn't taken the test of wearing the Brow; if he had, either he would have worn it yesterday in the arena, or he would be dead already. I turned to other tomes with similar bindings, and began to see a kind of church history scattered among the volumes. A slight crumbling sound made my body twitch. I spun around, scanning the enormous empty space behind me. The reading lectern by the cases faced the wall, and the books were too heavy to hold under the light without support. I was starting to dislike my present course of study. But nothing moved in the temple now that I faced the darkness, and the idea of checking an armload of tomes past the guards struck me as possessed of certain difficulties. I turned back to read, but resolved to remain more alert.

Almost at once, I hit the jackpot. Some chronicler from the twelfth or thirteenth century took the occasion of a church succession to not only mention the Brow, but to describe it in glowing tones. "Oh wondrous Brow! What sword can match your keen beauty?..." I started skimming through the poetry, this lonely scribe sounded like he had fallen in love. "...of triune bands, argent silver winding in perfection with greened orikhalc and crimson gold... each of the seven perfect heights above the triune bands, a gem set as if grown from seed..." then a great deal of description of the individual gems, together with more poetry about the alleged powers of the Brow. I got a bit dizzy trying to keep it all together. I looked around again at the darkness, still feeling as if watched, and then decided to risk the sacrilege. Not my temple anyway. I took out a thin, sharp blade and carefully cut through the two pages that held the description of the Brow. I stowed them away feeling like a thief.

I thought it was high time to go, but then my eye fell on a description of the conclave of preachers, the meeting this scribe had written the Brow into. I saw the words "reek and smoke" and also "sizzle of burning skulls" and my eye was drawn to the start of the passage. Evidently, the old patriarch of the church had died and the greatest preachers of the Mark had gathered to claim the title of Highforge.

So then did Knarg Spineslammer fall as well, and his charnel flesh dropped lifeless onto the heap of the other untrue claimants, whose bodies were no doubt repulsed—even in death—at the touch of him who was whispered to have garruk blood. Yet they all received their meted fate for daring to wear the Brow though unworthy, and were blasted for stepping beyond their station. And so it was, amid the reek and smoke, when boisterous shouts of these warlike prelates had long since dwindled into choking screams under the sizzle of burning skulls, so it was that Tel Amaren, the youngest curate of his Healer faction, in humbly fulfilling his duty to keep the meeting chamber clean, did pick up the Brow as he carried the fallen scepters and symbols and censors and roods of those who had died. And lo, even as he carried more than he could in the fervent call of his task; he did without thought carelessly place the Brow for a moment upon his head, somewhat aslant. The assembled other curates and acolytes saw at once, and cried out and drew back in horror at his fatal mistake. Yet behold! Amaren was unharmed, though he did wish to slay himself when apprised of his error. And the assembled survivors of the Charnel Testing did come, and Amaren all unwilling was forced to wear the deadly circlet again, and so was declared Highforge that very day. And all unwilling was he the wisest and most devout of all Elven memory...

I laughed so loud I had to straighten up, and caught the fleeting movement from above, on the ceiling. A scuttling shape the size of a pony, which gathered itself upside-down and then hurtled across the space at me. I leaped backwards and into a roll, and heard the thunk of a spear into the lectern. I came to my feet with the *noun-chakas* in hand, a honed reflex. All to the good, for the thing moved after me without any recovery time from its leap. I had a flash of hardness, speed and six legs; my knees went to dough, and I retreated even as I swung the hafts. I caught the thing flush above its waist and my weapon rebounded so hard from the armored skin that I was nearly hit. Four legs to walk and two to strike, I was dodging automatically as it came silently onward.

Like most Elves, I couldn't stand the sight of insects, the mindless grouped nature of them assailed me. But no elf I'd ever spoken with had seen one of the hobgoblins of our childhood tales, a giant Bug like this. I jogged backwards trying to get ahold of my panic. It came on smoothly over the minor obstacles of broken wood and uneven floor. That awful head, swiveled in all directions with gem-eyes sparkling dark green in patches of the moonlight. But the crowning obscenity for me was the sight of a spear in its hands; oddly worked, short with multiple wicked edges and a loop-handle for its claw.

I half-stepped into the edge of another hole, larger and deeper; the scent from the black earth made my eyes swim and I fell on my back to avoid falling in. I rolled over and heard the scuttling to one side. Rising, I used the double-hafts to block the spear, but the nether claw came hard on its heels and raked my ribs. Screaming with the fiery pain of it, I turned and ran, looking to put the altar between us. Bad move—it came directly over it and I didn't gain a step away. The pain in my side was flaring higher, and I sensed the touch of venom spreading, burning, numbing me. I lashed with my weapon up at its torso and scored a glancing hit—to my surprise, I knocked it entirely over, off the altar and on its side. I gauged it would stretch eight or nine feet end to end, yet the bug felt as if it weighed less than a hound.

It righted at once and bored in again, now with a clicking, chittering sound that got down into my spine and started rooting about. I fumbled with a holster-pouch and drew forth a small gem—really a construct of hollow crystal—and threw it down on the floor between us. It burst with a blast of brilliant light, bright enough to my side; the guards would probably see, but no help for that now. Facing the giant bug, the effect was like staring into a lightning-flash, and I figured with all that eye surface, it could be even worse. I wasn't wrong—clicking like a washboard, the thing fell back and curled into a writhing ball of limbs and chitin. I knew the effect didn't last long on human eyes, and was in no mood to take chances. I turned at a half-run, and immediately stumbled over a broken bench—what idiot said they weren't dangerous? I recovered my balance near another hole in the floor—or perhaps it was one I'd already seen. But I was teetering directly over it now, and noticed two things I hadn't before.

It did not end. It wasn't a divot or pit. It was a tunnel through the earth.

And another insect was coming up from the depths, chittering back to its partner.

Before I could regain my balance, it came within reach and stabbed out with its spear, taking me in the left shoulder and hooking back into my neck and jaw. I slapped out with the *noun-chakas*, kept always in motion—another hard-learned habit. The haft snapped clean through its foreleg at a narrow joint corresponding to a wrist, and the spear clattered to the floor. But with four more legs it continued to climb and I staggered back barely beyond the reach of its other fore-claw.

I stumbled, reeling away towards the door closest to the cases, opposite where I entered. My right side had no feeling, and my right leg was starting to be very uncooperative. I practically dragged it and there was no chance on earth I could make it through the door in time. But I heard the sounds of guards approaching, calling to each other—Argens bless those worthy citizens! I banged into the wooden portal and was through into a night that seemed unusually cool.

My vision hazed, surely I had a fever. Dimly I heard people shouting to each other, no one seeing anything unusual. Yet there I lay on the stone outside, bleeding to death through my black costume. Were they blind not to see me prostrate there? Or actually, slightly moving... very numb, head wouldn't turn to look, and could feel the impact of my feet being dragged. The monsters had taken me after all.

There's a small roof over my head—not a tunnel? I suspect I've rolled onto my back, though I am on fire now and the sweat is making it hard to see through the mask eyes. I can feel my strength ebbing and the weapon drops from my hand. A voice nearby says "*intakta volar*" and then I know I'm dreaming. Because a kindly uncle's face looks down on me and says "It's over."

$$\oplus \ \oplus \ \oplus$$

Even as I started to rouse I could feel in every muscle and bone, it was among the best naps I had ever taken. Dream gradually moved to consciousness in perfect rhythm, very centered. I felt languor and control at the same time; I could awaken as I chose, when I chose. And I chose to awaken, smiling beneath the dried sweat of my mask.

The tightness of the swath bandages on my ribs, and the binding around my lower jaw and neck, were the only physical report I had of my wounds. I felt no burning or pain, and I sensed there were no scars underneath, though the bloody splotches insisted otherwise. But beyond that, all the minor aches and stiffness that always beset one after sleep—whether in the business of bruising the body or not—were completely absent. I had not felt this good on first awakening since I was a child.

"You've come back, good," said that gentle voice, "I told you it was over, at first, but when your fever set in I had a few moments of doubt."

I turned my head and saw at once that I was in the small shed south of the chapel, more of a lean-to with one side open to the foundation pit. It was still night, though lighter than I expected. I guessed I had passed out for an hour or two. There on a wooden box sat the preacher, and in a flash I recognized all of him at once—the curate of the newly-restored reverence of Telhol, the man who held his seat at the arena table when that monstrous beast plunged from the sky. The cleric that those idiot guards had brought with them to exorcise the ghost. My worst enemy, unless you count me.

I froze, could not feel my weapon on my waist anywhere; there it lay about midway between us. My second thought was for my mask; I raised my hand to the bandages on my jaw.

"Forgive me," said the preacher, "My work is generally quite effective without touch but I have a long history with aid of a more physical nature. The bandages were needful, soaked with moss-resin in the event that the venom you had ingested grew again. I did my best not to remove your mask. But I'm afraid I can tell," he finished with a small smile, "that you are not really blonde."

I stared in disbelief. This human claimed to have healed me—I *know* I was badly hurt—and not to have looked at who I was? Part of me wanted to lunge for the *noun-chakas*, another part wanted to run for it. But I couldn't tell how powerful his spells would be, or how fast he was. Risking a husky whisper to disguise my true voice, I asked "How long?"

He cocked his head a moment, then nodded as comprehension came to him. "I see—not a wound to your throat then?" I shook my head and he grinned, looking out the shed to the sky. "You first came, from there—" he said, gesturing at the chapel behind my head, "an hour or so past midnight. Yesterday."

"Yesterday!" I sat up as if the bed had become hot, and instantly every ounce of well-being left my body. I sagged back, feeling as if only my feet and knees were normal, but everything higher was almost empty. He surged up and came to help ease me back down—I was weaker than a wet reed and could not fight him. No wonder he seemed unconcerned—I was probably drugged.

"Forgive me, sir," he pleaded, "your wounds I was able to repair, but you lost a great deal of blood. Those tears were designed to kill that way. Like claws, but also..." he stood over me as I lay back, at the same distance I had seen in my dream. "Please, try to rest."

"To be clear," the cleric said, holding up his hand to forestall me, "I mean to say the sun has risen and set twice since I found you." I looked at the sky now, and realized it was indeed getting darker. Two days! I had never slept more than five hours at a stretch since becoming an adult—but why would he lie? I snarled inwardly at myself to be quiet.

Gradually, my head cleared and I regained some balance. I lay on my cot—or in truth, I realized, his—and regarded this calm, almost diminutive human. He sat easily with one hand on a knee and regarded me in return, a gentle smile through his brown beard and not a shred of visible unease at hosting a masked man in the shadow of monsters. What did he know? How much was he a part of this? I shook my head a moment later—that last was nonsense. The man had healed me. I hated the thought as soon as I had it.

Part of me still counseled a sprint—I might faint, but there was no way he could stop me with the lean-to open on one side. The little man seemed quite content to sit and look at me, mildly curious but neither nervous nor apprehensive. I guessed he felt now as I had when I first woke up. Not powerful but in control: at peace, I realized. I insisted to myself he was lying, about the time I had been out, about not seeing my face under the mask. I looked into his eyes, brown like his hair, and saw two points of rock, not sharp flints but steady, unchanging granites. I sensed he had seen much more than his simple robe and rope belt implied, and that he had already made up his mind about telling the truth, long before we met.

"Guards," I hissed in my whisper-voice, "looking for me."

"As to that," he said with a smile, "I cannot be sure. I would guess they saw the same bright flash that I did, and perhaps heard a shout or scream. My pallet is closer than their posts, and I don't believe any

80

of them saw you, or me as I approached. I brought you here and did what I could." The preacher paused, still smiling kindly, and added, "If you are asking whether the guards came here, the answer is no. They have grown quite accustomed to my presence, and while I don't read minds, I think they know I would tell them of any outlaws." He gazed on me with a fond expression then, as if he knew me well. "I have seen no outlaws these days, and so had nothing to report."

"If I may be so bold," he continued, "you are the one called Feldspar, yes?" I saw no point in lying, so I nodded, and he continued looking warmly at me. "Yes, I could sense it, you have that same way about you. A follower of Astor, the Perilsgroom; you certainly honored him in there. I have had the privilege to accompany—and heal—stealthics before. I feel confident, you would be of no interest to those hunting law-breakers." We sat awhile in silence and the fullness of night blanketed the view. The preacher swung an iron bar with a pot of broth back over his little fire, getting it ready for me I guessed. More drugs, I screamed silently, but the tide of battle was slipping. I felt a little more comfortable discussing questions delicate and horrible. Enemy or not, he was my only source, and I had to know.

First things first; I whispered, "Saved my life, payment." As expected, he shook his head without comment. But I had pride. "Something you need—anything," I hissed.

The human shrugged and pursed his lower lip. "Peace on earth."

I barked a laugh in my normal voice, but stopped when I saw his gaze. Noticing the foundation, I gestured and whispered, "What are you building?"

"A chapel. Very slowly." He rose and dusted his robe, pointing to a plan sketched on a parchment pinned to the wall. I could see at a glance this would be a very modest establishment; no room for a large statue, none called for on the sketch. Even so, the amount of stone and mortar piled outside was inadequate even to finish shoring the foundation. "Once the worship of Telhol was permitted, I petitioned the Fire Grip and he gave me license to build here, which seemed fitting. I have received some excellent advice from masons who have lent their time, and I direct any volunteers who come by, when they can."

I pointed to the enormous, ruined chapel looming to one side. "Has there been, has anything—".

The cleric shook his head, "Not a sign, except I overheard the guards found a spear with an odd handle. If you can forgive my curiosity, what did you encounter in that church?"

I hated to admit the fact now, but I knew I could trust this man. Not his fault he'd killed me last week. "Giant bugs."

The man at last raised both brows, though not in fear. "Ah. Insectirs." He placed both hands on his knees. "Not very pleasant for your race. Or any other, of course; but Elves, I understand, find insects of all kinds particularly unnerving. That was always Rainor's reaction." He drifted off in reverie, and I strained to recall where I had heard that name before. Rainor was... someone important, recently raised to power, an alchemist or wizard of some kind. I thought of Yula, the usurper, and my spine suddenly cooled.

I started to whisper, but my voice choked and I had to try again. "Your name?" The quiet little human returned my gaze, and nodded as if in admission, "I am Kama."

I could not restrain a tight laugh of derision. "Kama! Is that why you don't fear outlaws—you've named yourself after one." The little man stirred the broth into a bowl as if I had not spoken. "I mean, he was a Telholian, like... you... but, he was... he assaulted two wizards in broad daylight. There was—a price on his head."

I trailed off as my brain caught up to my mouth. It was the emperor Viridian, of course, who had outlawed Kama, and his companions, after that incident more than a year ago. Politics, I didn't read about it closely. Kama was declared guilty of a spectacular assault, branded a dangerous outlaw along with his adventurer-companions. And the sect had been banned for as long as I could remember. I was perfectly willing to believe what I had heard, of course; when this Telholian flushed me from the warehouse, my rage and the old news of the sect's villainy fitted perfectly. The removal of Viridian meant nothing to me until today. I looked on the man and suspected how evil the old regime must have been, to persecute this inoffensive fellow. And yet—I propped up on an elbow as he brought me the broth. My head swam but I waited, and he with me, until my hands were steady enough to hold the bowl.

He turned to go, saying "You'll find that difficult enough to manage, without leaving your mask on. I will just—"

"The fight," I rasped, stopping him at the edge of the lean-to. "I thought, followers of Telhol, forbidden."

"Your broth will get cold. Drink, and in a time I'll return to speak further."

He turned the corner out of sight, and I heard the sounds of a small man struggling with a large stone. Pushing up my mask I drank off the broth in a single gulp, only remembering afterwards it might be sleep-drugged. Part of me recognized all such fears as childish, but I had no stomach to sleep any more after hearing how much time I had missed. No matter, hunger ruled me now. I slowly walked to the fire, refilled the bowl and drank it off again, looking over to the chapel of Argens Demonbender and not knowing whether to hope to see something at the doors or not. I was still quite dizzy and weak, so I made my way back to the bed intending to sit but winding up on my back again. I doubted I would be leaving this area tonight, no matter how urgent the business.

After a decent interval there was a knock on the wall. I flipped down my mask as Kama returned. He checked the broth-pot, nodded with approval and sat again on the box. I couldn't hate him anymore, at least not much, but I disliked being further in his debt. I started to rise, gesturing that he should lie down. But the man hopped up to hold me gently back, and pointed to a roll of blankets in the corner below my feet. "Please, sir, do not concern yourself with these amenities. I have slept much worse on many an occasion." I knew that if one-tenth the tales told of Yula and his companions were true, he was not boasting.

"The fight," I prompted in a gentle hiss.

"The Imperial Wizards Balen'th and F'liths had power, wealth and the favor of their emperor," Kama replied steadily, his face lit now by the small campfire. "As many of your noble classes do, their ages stopped in the prime of their lives; they had in short, every advantage one could wish. Yet they feuded. I later heard their fight that day was just another chapter of a personal war that had lasted for decades." He stopped awhile, and when he resumed, his voice was lower, the tone more halting. "I knew none of this, until I met them for the first time, on a crowded street in the center of Argens itself."

"Did you attack first?" I asked; he looked at me strangely before answering.

"They attacked each other. The feud, of course, more important than any delay, or any consideration for the innocent people crammed into the square." He drew a deep breath, and something entered his tone that sounded like steel. "Have you ever seen a wizard's duel, Feldspar? They are quite rare, and rightfully so. The mages, even in this honor-drunk empire, are well organized. They study under masters, test themselves constantly. Each one knows his place, and the outcome of a challenge is foreseen. But for these two, the feud was all that mattered."

"It was mid-day, the hour of market. I saw mothers with their children set on fire, as the two of them howled curses and aimed their staves at one another. None could resist them, even the soldiers and guards fled. A merchant's scribe not ten steps from me was struck by some wave of eldritch force, bright yellow and sharp, and he simply disappeared. I never knew what became of him." For the first time, I saw real anger on his face. He was unable to continue.

"I don't understand," I said quietly, "you weren't involved?"

"I stopped them."

"You!" I forgot to whisper as I looked on this little man. "You just said no one could stop them. Aren't you Telholians sworn to peace."

He nodded, but for a time did not answer. At last he said, "I can tell you do not trust me, Feldspar. I know our reputation under Viridian was not flattering. I am indeed sworn to peace, which is, the goal of peace for all. Telhol did not stand meekly by when innocents were threatened. Our training, our... faith, is that we must... interpose." He looked up at me then and by the small firelight he held my eyes. "We are not so different, you know. Astor never made fun of Telhol as he did with so many other more powerful heroes. They both sought to take the risk upon themselves, yes? To simply fight, to raise one's fist or weapon at the first provocation, to seek combat rather than victory, you would scorn that as the act of a mere soldier. Am I correct?"

I nodded, and he considered, "Fighting is failure. Morinack always said as much."

84

"Morinack? The halfling, the Emperor's Hand?"

"I told you, I sense a similar approach, what I have heard tell of you and what I saw of him." He shrugged, and resumed his tale, "We who follow Telhol seek peace, starting from ourselves and spreading as far as we can bring it. You fight only when you must. Telhol teaches that we must never need to fight; perhaps a small difference, but in that teaching is a kind of power. So I stopped them."

It began to come back to me as I thought about it. "I remember," I said. Not the official declarations which came with the pronouncement of his guilt, but what the tavern-folk had repeated, all the many mouths and ears up from the capital to Cryssigens, and I repeated the tale now by the firelight.

"The preacher of Telhol, people said, knelt in the square and prayed. And from him grew a circle of white force, spreading out through the innocent persons, shielding them from the sorceries arcing in both directions. The wizards shouted their frustration and hurled ever-more powerful bolts, using all the resources at their disposal as seldom before. Yet still the circle grew, and when it enveloped the two wizards, they became incapable of even speaking the words of power." I remembered too, each mage fell to the muddy street, getting filthy and somewhat trampled by the panicking crowd. By the time order was restored, the Telholian preacher had vanished into infamy. The rare members of a tiny cult were confirmed in their reputation for outlawry, but above all the one called Kama. A hundred thousand pieces of silver for his imprisonment.

"They called it an assault," Kama said, "evidently because I dared to prevent elves of noble rank from doing as they saw fit." I looked on him, no longer feeling distrust or spite, but now a kind of fear. I was helpless and weak with a man who defeated high imperial mages for a living. And who exorcised spirits. My curiosity got the better of me.

"Telhol," I hissed, "fought the undead. Destroyed them. Not peace."

Kama shook his head. "You misunderstand. The animate remains of those who have died—gaunts, ombrumae, revenants—are a prime sign of Despair's influence on the world. They have been dragged far beyond the state of nature by a curse. Telhol brought peace, seeing that such is the natural state of a child of Hope. The proper state of an undead being is death. We do not fight them—we restore them."

I watched his face closely but saw no sign that he thought of his latest service in this area. Until an hour ago I had known this man as an enemy, but that was personal. Even my inflated sense of self had not extended this far. Viridian was right, a part of me muttered, to hunt this much power in one man. Yet there he sat, sipping perhaps one fourth the broth I had already gulped down. He might have owned a little more in his clothes and personal effects than I carried on me in commission gems. And his face spoke of peace.

I could tell I'd be with him at least another night, and I knew my own curiosity would never hold out. I rustled in my holster and took out the cut pages, gesturing to him.

"What do you know," I whispered, "about the Brow of the Ecclesiast?"

⊕ ⊕ ⊕

I never could get rid of the little man. He was there when I awoke again in mid-morning, fed me, chatted pleasantly about small things. When I stood up, he stood by, watched my progress and agreed I could likely make my own way that evening, if I truly wished. I truly did.

But even when he left me, to rest while he worked with pathetic patience on his building, even then I was not alone. Everything Kama said, about peace and honest dealings, what made an act just or a man worthy—it was all upside down and all exactly right. He was as gentle and tolerant of my views as Ekatarinye had been, but it galled me as much as the pompous tutors of the Hopeforgers had. And I, who had never given a tinker's damn about what happened beyond the range of my vision with any other man; I found myself staggering outside the lean-to after sunset, to help him with the stone.

Without my tunic shirt or bandages I looked less noticeable, even with my mask on; perhaps just another day-laborer come to volunteer. Kama was trying to wrestle the cubic granite of the cornerstone onto the rollers, and moving slowly I could help him brace it and set the logs in place. He did most of the pushing but by the time we had moved the cursed thing ten feet I was bathed in sweat. The dizziness only came twice though as I held myself in check, and we stopped several times, chatting again while catching our breath.

"Why not find the Brow?" I whispered while panting, which was truly difficult but old habits do not die easy.

"I did not say that," Kama replied passing me a water skin. "I said I wish it had never been made."

"My job, to find it."

He smiled in a friendly way. "You must do as you think best, of course. And whether you locate it or not, Hope will be served by your sincere efforts."

"You fear power in another's hands?"

"I have some fear of power, yes, in anyone's hands, perhaps most my own," Kama replied, and the words I would have taken as fluff or flattery from any other mouth sounded irrefutable from his. He had indeed wielded power, he knew something about this. I had never doubted the rightness of this commission, or any that I had taken before.

"I heard a bard in the taverns, last year," I said quietly, "insisted your miracle, the Ring of Peace, was not seen in the Lands since Telhol himself used it. At the Battle of the Razor."

Kama looked almost sheepish. "I only know that when it was done, I was as weak as you were the hour you came to me. The others, Yula and the rest of our party, got me safely away. And became outlaws mostly because of me too. It's certainly good to have friends. I hope you have some."

I ignored that. "The priestess is worthy," I whispered, "not just beautiful, wants peace for the Mark."

Kama shrugged briefly, with a small smile that said "perhaps". I got a bit angry then.

"Should there be no Overlord? Are we better without a leader? Fires, assassinations, theft and crime!" my voice rose to normal tones again—I could not just leave his words outside me as I had with others. I thought I was beyond this tutoring stage.

Kama pondered this a while, and nodded. "It is true, we have seen more crime this past year—theft, assault, some murder. This past week I have heard of a new crime, the taking of hostages. Folks from every precinct have been disappearing; most think it is the guilds or

Cups exerting pressure on rivals. I cannot say why this happens. But consider—with a strong Mark, we had slavery, drugs sold openly, and the constant threat of rebellion. This marvelous crown you seek was used to spur such revolt in ages past, time and again. And I mislike that it was created in part by powers not born to Hope."

That was a point, part of me insisted. But I was in a mood—I got up and slammed another roller in front of the stone, as he plied the iron wedge-bar to move it forward. My brain at last found the riposte it was looking for. "At least she will take the risk on herself."

Kama finished his push, and considered this while I triumphantly recovered the back roller and brought it front. When it was ready, he still didn't move, so I looked up at him.

"Do you mean," he said carefully, "the Mark would be better off with W'starrah Altieri dead?"

I was stunned. "You don't think she is worthy?" I hissed.

"Feldpar," Kama said, leaning in towards me and dropping his voice as if someone in the ruined temple were listening. "Worthy, of what?"

"We know," he continued as he resumed levering the stone, "that some who tried to don the circlet were burned to death. I know from the histories, upon success for a new Highforge, the chronicles tell of a rebellion or civil war within a year."

I listened as I moved more logs in front, then joined him in the back as we neared the spot he had chalked on the ground. "But," I gasped with my shoulders backed against the stone, "the Brow... once chose... a Telholian. Good sign."

"Do you think so?" he replied with a small smirk. "I'm gratified to hear your good opinion of the sect, sir." The man had an annoying habit of setting me at odds with myself. "You told me it was first crafted by this elven lord Mart'l'n long ago—he was trying to unify a church. I ask—was the Brow effective towards that end?"

I was so surprised I stopped pushing.

"How do we know it will work to the ends intended by W'starrah Altieri?" Kama continued, "She is aflame with the desire to do great good, I have no doubt. I pray that she will. Meanwhile there is good we can see, immediately before us," the preacher concluded. We both took no more breath for talk then, as we heaved and maneuvered the block into position, kicking the last rollers out like arrows from a bow as it thunked into place. I leaned over the top of it like a table and Kama patted my back, saying, "Thank you."

When I could stand up again without dizziness, I returned to get my tunic and weapon to leave. Back at the foundation, Kama was standing halfway down into the pit and quietly chiseling into the back of the cornerstone. As I approached, he stood up to admire his effort. On the back of the granite block was now a clear, even "K". He was evidently finished—no long inscription with full name, year, the glory of Telhol, and so forth. Just a letter, which would soon be covered by the wall stones behind it anyway. Small and real; just like him.

He held out the chisel and hammer to me and I warded with my hands. But he insisted, saying "It's because of you this cornerstone is in place." I thought about things under the surface, and taking risks, about having a little fun. And I remembered, much as I hated the training in the Hopeforger school, I did like hitting stones. I took the tools, got down in the pit as Kama left, and carefully lined up the chisel beneath his mark. I took three careful strikes, then two finishing strokes, and I was done. Beneath the "K" was now a strong, less neat but clearly marked letter "J". Kama looked, grinned, then chuckled at the riddle. I laid the tools on top and smoothed the surface. "Good stone," I whispered, "good stone."

It was full dark and my feet were practically flinching with the need to go. I held out my arm, reluctantly, in gratitude, and he took it—without casting some miracle on me, though I held my breath. Inside, I swore to do him some great favor without ever laying eyes on him again. As I moved towards the edge of the compound, I could see him raise his arm after me, like a farewell though I feared it was a blessing.

Guards don't generally spot anyone trying to leave a forbidden place.

As I moved across the inner city again, I felt some distant aches of disuse in my limbs, but my head stayed marvelously clear. I seemed to get better as I went, back into my life again (and further from the preacher's influence). From a rooftop overlooking The Boards I could see my new neighborhood was more lit than before, and I sensed trouble. Parties of everyday folk with torches walked the side streets, several more along the boardwalk looking out to the river. A large solid elf with a pretty young lady sat on the stoop of my house with his head in his hands. I slipped down into an alley and quickly changed, stashing my work clothes beneath the house itself. Then I walked back a few blocks to come down my street in the normal way.

Droke Staveshaver rose as 'Lashi noticed me coming, and I exchanged words with him directly for the first time.

"Mr. Simith, you've come back."

"Ah, yes," I drawled, "a business trip, back to Tamar, citizen Staveshaver, couldn't be helped. How may I—"

"It's Keilee," the young priestess blurted out, and I took a wary glance in her direction but tried not to meet her eyes.

"Keilee? I saw her, ahm, three mornings ago, the arena day, yes. I told her I would not need dinner that even—"

"Then she is not with you," Droke's words fell like a hammer and I feared the worst.

"She's been taken! I know it!" the lovely girl cried and Droke turned at once to her.

"Talishaya, none of that. She's run off before—"

"I say, she has?" I exclaimed and he turned back heavily to me. I regretted the words as soon as I saw his eyes.

"Overnight, yes. At times. I work, sir, as does my wife, and now that my eldest is apprenticed to the Stargazers…" his voice broke, and I could hear his pride cracking with it. "Keilee is a rather active child."

I held up my hands in apology. "I quite understand, sir. I feel responsible here, somewhat. I, ahm, was perhaps a bit short with the girl that morning…" My mouth was running on, and before I knew it I had dug a pit for myself. Again. The lovely girl took my arm and I had no choice but to meet her gaze.

"Please, kind sir, if there's anything you can do."

A miracle being cast? My love for a beautiful face? Boredom after three days of enforced inactivity? I could probably have stood there three more days and not figured it out. At that moment, I just bowed to her, shook the father's iron-gripping hand, and saw them off before going inside. Less than five minutes later, I had washed up, grabbed a few bites of food the missing girl had provided, and after some deliberation, created a mate for the broken chair in the living room.

Then I strode around the corner to the tavern. Noudhal was out with a search party; the only fellow I knew was the brick-hauler Giurid, tending bar for the moment. Less parties to a conversation always brings clarity, and he had no doubt whatever as to the meaning of it all.

"It's the Red House," he asserted forcefully, "pushing the rest of us around getting ready for the vote."

"Do you mean, they are taking hostages to influence the selection of the new Overlord?"

"What else?"

"But Keilee is Droke's daughter, and he's a Red House man."

His brow furrowed briefly with the effort of this little roadblock; he had been speaking of the matter generally, preparatory to a lecture about law and order. He made a dismissive gesture, giving up on the annoying fact. "She must have gotten in the way, poor little brat. And anyway, who can understand how criminals act? This is essactly why," he lisped a bit, tipping what he had been doing on such a quiet night in the bar, "we need a leader in this Sity." I nodded in time with him and assured he must be right. Then I left with a sinking feeling in my gut. I knew I had to do something, and soon, but I was lost for a lead. And the quest for the Brow ate at me—whatever doubts Kama had managed to instill, I had taken the commission. Find it, or die trying, that was my own code though no one had asked.

I strolled along the river-boards, half-heartedly looking while trying to think. Giurid was right about one thing; the acts of these criminals defied common sense. I exchanged words with some searchers I met; very few of those kidnapped were of any rank. Ransom was not likely, and I knew that though the election process was complex, there was simply no way the taking of a barrelmaker's urchin was going to sway the vote. Murder for fun? Trying to start panic, perhaps—but again, the takings were widespread and often folks of little repute. It occurred to me that some of the poor often went missing—the odorous beggar occasioned surprise in his usual haunts whenever he returned. It might be that something had always been happening, only now more so.

I needed a criminal mind to figure this out. And despite the opinion of some, I didn't have one. But there was one criminal I knew. I headed towards the dock gaol to ask for the prisoner Farlo.

Near the mouth of the Tepid within sight of the Palace above, steps led down from the boardwalk right to the shore, to a tower of reinforced oak set against the steep bank to hold those who have committed crimes in the precincts around The Boards. As luck would have it, Beirill was on duty tonight; justice never sleeps. He loomed behind the desk sitting nearly on a level with me standing, and asked my business as if I were a stranger to him. With an inward reminder that I was, I kicked myself into motion from the doorway and approached.

"Ah yes, guard Dekentar Beirill is it? I was told you had a prisoner here, guilty of an assault some half a week or so ago."

"He's here," he replied, "No one to speak for him, so he awaits trial."

"Is he, ahm, likely to be convicted may I ask?"

He nodded, "No one to speak for him, and we saw clear signs of a fight all around. We think he was part of a gang, perhaps just picked on someone out of their league for once; the others ran, probably pursued by their target, just before we arrived."

"I see," I mused, amused. "So in truth, you have no, what would you call it, no accusation?"

"It's clear he was in a fight," Beirill was becoming a little testy. "I think they may have wounded the fellow they attacked, and later were able to turn the tables on him. Did you see anything? Are you come to swear out a complaint?"

"Complaint? Ahm no, I was rather hopeful I might, that is, that it would be permitted me to see and speak with him."

The warrior's instincts rose at that and he frowned darkly. "Why? Either you are the one he assaulted—or perhaps you know his confederates?"

"I! Faith of the First, no, sir. I assure you, I have no truck with law-breaking of such low purpose." And this was the truth, for I only bent laws and then only with a very high purpose. But I needed to bend a bit more now, I could see, if I were to gain an interview. I scratched mentally for a course.

"It's simply that—well, I've been to see the new healer in the city, the man of Telhol." This held Beirill's interest, I could see; pretty ironic if that man opened this door for me. "I've heard him speak, ahm, about justice and mercy, you know, and I must say, Captain," a little flattery wouldn't hurt, "I have been very moved, indeed, deeply affected by his words. I come to think, rather, that every one of us, perhaps, is not beyond improvement. So I thought I might, that is, if I can speak with this fellow, and see whether he has, ahm, repented of his ways, well then I might be persuaded to stand for him."

Beirill went from not following my words to not believing his ears. "You would post a surety for his appearance at trial?"

"Well, if I am convinced, that is, you know, if I could just speak with him."

"But you've never even seen him!"

"Ah yes, well, the best deeds are often done outside one's circle of friends, yes? These are the truly good deeds, I believe the preacher would say..." and so droning on, I realized from his face that I had him. He shook his head, but rose to take the keys and lead me back to the cells.

The corridor was narrow, and the walls, floor and ceiling had iron straps, to inhibit magical energy. We were walking directly into the side of the riverbank, and I realized we were likely underground, in a carved tunnel of sorts. Of course no windows, so the lantern Beirill held became the only source of light. The hallway ended in a locked door, through which was a keyhole-shaped ending with cells opening out along eight different paths from the central circle. Only one was occupied; the thin elf at the back sat up at the sound of our entrance and blinked in the sudden light. Beirill hung the lantern on the wall and left me to him, saying "You can have a few minutes, I'll be right outside." He closed the outer door to the cell-chamber behind him, and I realized he wanted no part of my altruism. Neither did I, but Farlo was the only lead I had.

He rose and shuffled towards the bars; I could see his nose was high and thin as a shelf-divider. I turned the lantern so that he, not I, was illuminated, and let some time pass while I thought of what to say. It wasn't long, but Farlo was a chatty sort.

"Did Barkarr send you?" I marveled at the fellow's lack of guile. He didn't recognize the intended victim of his boss' crime; maybe if I showed him the back of my head it would jog his memory.

"My good fellow," I drawled, "I find it in my power to free a prisoner today, if I can be assured, that is, of his worth."

Farlo just gaped in my direction through the bars. I prompted him.

"Would you like to be free?" He nodded. "And would you return, for trial when the day comes?" Another nod—this was easy enough even for him. No chance of that, I knew, but the cost of his surety would be worth it—if he knew anything.

"You wouldn't, perhaps, go missing as so many others have these days."

That caught him by surprise—the thug stopped breathing and didn't move for two full beats. Then he recognized me, with nearly a whine on his features. So, he knew something; if I let him go, he'd be worth following.

I rapped on the outer door and Beirill opened. When I asked about the amount of the surety I could see by his face that he named an inflated figure to make me balk. I promptly announced that this was acceptable, and there he was caught. With murder on his face, he unlocked Farlo's cell and prodded him back down the hallway to the desk. Fortunately, the city administration had heard some things about modern finance. I was able to sign a chit for the amount, drawn on my generous employer's bank the next day. Beirill looked it over with a sour face, sat down and brusquely waved us away without a word. I easily forgave him as I left with his only prisoner; guards hate having nothing to guard.

The walk up to The Boards with Farlo was among the most uncomfortable moments of my new life. I had nothing to say to the reedy little dope, and couldn't wait for him to give me the slip. But I should have known, he was unable to cope with new situations. He galumphed along beside me up every wooden step, and on the street level by the light of the torch-post he just stood there and looked at me as if I might give him a treat.

"So then," I said with an effort at cheer, "I shall depend on your honor, sir, to return for trial." Farlo stood there as if I had not yet said the magic word. "And I would like to see you tomorrow," I temporized, "at… ahm, in front of the Grog's Lees tavern. At noon, on the moment, do you hear me?" He nodded, sensing a lie he could actually understand, and smiled at me. "Or else," I added in Simith's best effete air, "I shall be most disappointed in you." Farlo nodded in complete agreement as to what my state should be tomorrow at noon. I nodded back, he bowed, I waved him off, he bowed again, and then turned to go. I watched him for a few steps, then put my hands behind my back, started to whistle (which I did very badly) and strolled off at a right angle to his course.

In twenty steps he was out of sight. In ten minutes I was in my work clothes and running across the rooftops towards the place he might have headed. I saw him exactly where he belonged, without so much as a single turn or alteration of speed. I felt sorry for Barkarr, if this was the level of his assistance.

I leaped between the closely-set roofs, practicing the art of landing on the quiet ball of each foot in my soft leather boots. Larger streets sometimes required a running vault, or perhaps descent to an alley and a bit of work to use shadows, but tonight there was little traffic, as Keilee's searchers had at last given up for sleep. I feared the worst for her, if she had fallen into the hands of people with as much mercy as Barkarr—or as much intelligence as Farlo.

He stopped at a corner between two shipping warehouses backed onto the river, and began looking about him with great caution. I sat above and across the street, also looking to all sides but seeing no one. I felt impatience, which threatens success, and tried to calm my nerves through breathing. With wonder I realized I was anxious, not for the Brow, for getting on with my great commission, but for a little girl. I had no warmth for Keilee, I was sure; perhaps a bit of admiration for her daring, and a little sympathy that her family could not attend her every change of mood. But she was real, a real person I had met; my last two dinners were from the larder she stocked for me. Since talking to that damned Kama, the prospect of finding the crown that could unite a Mark seemed somehow less appealing. Both involved risk in the service of Hope, both seemed hopeless right now. Recovering the Brow was a great good, but saving Keilee was a good that I could see.

At last Farlo issued a low, three-tone whistle and I tingled to realize he was signaling a compatriot. A few moments later the answering tones came and I pinpointed them from the upper window of one of the warehouses. On my belly I wormed back across my roof, rose and leaped a house further back, then worked my way around to come upon the warehouse from a blind side, climbing the wall. Whoever the lookout was had no art—I could hear him rustling about while I crossed the warehouse roof and from the gable I could see a bit of his head as he peered out the window. I briefly debating removing him, but aside from the delay, it would put a time-limit on my work; his recovery or the next shift, both indeterminate. Killing him was of course out of the question, too crude to be considered.

I slipped down the other side of the warehouse into a tar-black alley of packed wet earth slanting down to the river's edge. The smell of shipping and stagnant water-life was very strong. I walked down and back using my night-sight to pick out something unusual. Just an alley way, dark and muddy. Testing both warehouse walls for secret doors would take a month. But why not just walk into the warehouse anyway? I was starting to wonder if Farlo had tried to swim, when I noticed a small piece of ground that was folded under itself. As in, not ground but a patch of cloth, covered in silt near the base of one wall. The mucky cloth was fixed to wood, and by feeling about the edges I could lift the trap door. A ladder leading down gave me hope of a basement room where the thieves hid out between jobs. I descended to confirm this, ready to return with Beirill. The air was close and still, and instead of the sounds of a nearby gang of thieves I heard only a slow, steady drip from one side. I had to risk my target-lantern; the circle of light showed walls on three sides, the floor leading off in the wrong direction. A tunnel, then, slanting down. Toward the river's edge. Under it. To the old city.

I took a deep breath, then several more. Shuttering the lantern until it showed a patch of the floor no larger than my hand, I set out. My imagination, always a joy at such times, spent the moments showing me pictures of blades and spikes set into the ceiling at neck or eye level. Thrusting a forearm beyond my head did little to settle the matter—my mind simply pictured trip-wires, pit traps, even side tunnels (I congratulated myself on that last). I had to stop once or twice to catch my breath despite the lack of exertion; my heart was pounding, throwing too little blood around in my body for comfort. I took some time to examine the walls of the tunnel, and saw an unnerving mix of wood-braced wet earth, followed by patches of what could have been rubble or trash faced with thick uneven plaster, and a few spots of very strong and well-set stonework. The enormous weight of the river above showed in no more than a minor leak here and there, and the dark basalt in the stone was a kind I knew to be rare in this day. Gorgeous show-stone, thrown into a subterranean tunnel as if this were a major temple; a sign of value and respect, but interspersed with the plastered sections as if the builders were in a hurry.

The tunnel leveled off and I knew I was beneath the Tepid. I could no longer doubt I was headed for Old Cryss. That more than anything slowed my step, though now I had little chance of catching up to Farlo. I thought about turning back, when a small projection from one plastered wall caught my eye. It was a triangle at about waist level and it was the wrong color for stone. Stepping over to it, by the light of my small lantern I saw it was a piece of cloth thrusting from the crumbling plaster wall, rusty brown linen of great age. Something about it stirred the hair on my neck—then I realized it was open in the middle, and hemmed like the end of a sleeve. I backed away, looking up and down the wall's lumpy expanse as I added to my mental list of its ingredients. I turned and started to run, thanking Astor after a few dozen steps, that I was headed onward.

As the tunnel floor slanted up I returned to a walk again, and strained to hear. The light showed an end identical to the beginning, another ladder leading up. I stowed the lantern and ascended. Bracing my back against the wall I used both hands to gently crack the surface less than a half-inch. The light seemed brighter than day, but I held in the panic and waited for my vision to clear. If this end was guarded, things would not go well.

Ahead of me, the bottom of a jug and a cup; to one side, an open doorway and—praise Astor!—the heels of a pair of boots. There was a guard, but he was bored as guards often get, and watching down the street instead of attending to the trap door. I eased the *noun-chakas* from the holster, gathered my feet on the highest step and coiled up for action. I rose, shedding the trap door with my shoulders, and started the haft whirling as I stepped up. Three impacts in rapid succession—the trap door against the wall, my *noun-chakas* flush to his head, and the thug's body meeting the floor. I looked down the way he had watched, and saw only a thickly-shadowed avenue utterly lacking in light or movement. I checked his pulse, tied him and looked him over.

He could have been Farlo's cousin; no one looks smart when they're unconscious, but I doubted there would be much improvement when he awoke. He was an older elf, craggy features, unkempt and mussed from falling down without his hands; the neatest thing on him was his scimitar, still in its sheath. But there was no clever pass-key, or symbol around his neck, no secret word written backwards on his forehead. I sat him back near his jug and cup, trying to make it look like he'd fallen asleep. With his hands behind him. Nothing is perfect.

It wasn't until I stepped out of the doorway and into the street that I felt it. Cold, high, dark stone rose on all sides, so tall only a slice of the sky showed overhead—taller even than in the central section of the new city. The street was small, but I figured it was an alley; even so, the buildings loomed over me, aware and menacing. Either nothing was made of wood or it had long since rotted away. The cold of all that stone radiated into me, even the wind seemed brisk here. I stepped against one wall and slid down to the corner. The alley was set at an angle, and I couldn't see as much as I hoped. No sign of Farlo, no clue to any living thing. But I did see another avenue of high-built, solid, cold stone. Doorways were double, windows high and barred, roofs soared above me, every pillar and paving block seemed extra thick, yet not crude. And this street was wider, as broad as Altair Way. Yet I sensed the street was not the center of town, though it might lead there. I wondered if all of Old Cryss were like this, and I shivered.

To my left the broad street slanted back towards the river, nearer to the sea. Not likely Farlo would cross under the Tepid only to head back to it. Yet I had to force my steps to the right—the center of the Old City had supposedly been unoccupied for centuries. I clung to one side of the avenue, in a sweat though walking slowly and despite the cold. I only looked once at the roof-tops and couldn't bear the thought of taking to them. I put my mind to the source of this feeling, and realized I was passing grand public buildings, block after block. Huge structures with steps leading up, double-doors leading in, windows stretching two stories tall, flat or mildly peaked roofs, and domes. These were libraries, shrines, offices for posts long-since forgotten. But there were no homes. Every intersection—always angled, never square—only led to another broad avenue with grand architecture on both sides. The alley I first came from was the result of river-edge warehouses butting up against the rest. But I passed a dozen crossings and never saw a place where people lived. Even centuries ago, Old Cryss had been empty at night.

The smell was constant, pushing on me like a breeze; rank and aged. I recalled the tales of horrible sanitation, sewage running in the streets, sudden abandonment. One or two buildings were broken in or ruined with time, but overall the city emanated an awful sense of intactness, of utter solidity and emptiness. I was like most people— couldn't believe this big space was really uninhabited. I began to imagine the horrid undead that were thought to roam its streets, and part of me would have been relieved, just to know something else moved here besides me, and the chill wind.

And Farlo, I reminded myself, and those he was going to meet, and just maybe a little girl among the missing. And still alive. I picked up my pace and at the next corner saw to my left the crossing avenue opened up into an enormous space, a precinct surrounded by a low wall and filled with sights too numerous to take in. I ducked back behind the corner to think; this was the center of the Old City, and every ounce of me believed the place Farlo must have headed. I strained to remember—what did the third villain say to Barkarr when they fled? The piazzo. It was a just a word uttered in chaos, several days ago. Those blows to the head must have hurt more than I thought. Of course—the piazzo, center of the curse that destroyed Old Cryss. Where else.

I deliberately stepped around the corner and faced the sight, lying under the cloud-pinched moons two furlongs away. I looked at the low wall and the great shapes of the structures and statues beyond, and brought my mind to bear on the mortal danger of it. And Feldspar, who had been waiting for a week, chuckled up to the surface as I dwelt on the sheer peril. What had I done yet, among the living of Cryssigens, to compare with this? Get the Grip his gavel back, and leave a neat copy in place to sow mayhem among his enemies? Make a few bards sing for a month, cause a guard or two to want to pull me in. But ahead of me—curses, wreck, ancient traps, disease, undead, criminals, monstrous beings; everything that all the tales had told, waiting down there. The peril of the unknown beckoned me tonight. I was whole again, and slipped towards the wall with a bounce in my step and a grin under my mask.

I reached the end of the new avenue and waited for the clouds to cover the moons before crossing to the wall. Above me the stone street placard declared "Salva Way". The name stirred a dim whisper, as did the cross-route "Scapegrace Street", decorations of stories told to frighten me as a child. Now I was really here, and Feldspar tittered with delight. The moons briefly ducked behind a cloud bank and I sprinted half-bent across Salva's broad cobbles to take shelter beside the four-foot wall of cut brick. As the orbs cleared and a wave of light swept toward me, I turned to poke just my head above the masonry top and look straight into the place where bad dreams came from.

The open square was shaped like an uneven lozenge the size of a village. Within the walls, every inch not occupied by a building showed the interlocking hook-shaped tiles of ceramic and sectioned granite that gave the place its name. The sheer size of the open paved space filled me with wonder; by the passing of centuries the surface was cracked and pushed up in many places. Dotting the moonlit view were temples, a large garden with creeper-covered walls and gates, the central statue-podium where the eight Exemplars stood carved in twelve feet and more of polished serpentine.

To my left in the nook of the next corner was a small area ringed with a low, two-foot fence of metal spikes; I caught only a glimpse of the irregular rows of stone markers within and turned my head away with a snap. I had heard the stories, but hoped like most children that this one wasn't true. No such luck—they had really done it, those grand fools of long ago. So proud, so eager to show their spirit even in death, they had built a *kemetaria*, and allowed their bones to be put under the earth—an added challenge for their souls, to rise despite the odds and still attain heaven. Confident and sure, they had put their flesh into the ground, like the children of Despair. No wonder death had rained down on this place.

But now there was more. I caught slivers of shadow and the end-notes of dim echoes, back to the right, inside one of the largest and most intact temples on this side. It looked like a Stargazer facility, though not nearly as distinct as the modern building. The colored glass of its windows glowed with uneven lights. I hunched down the outer wall to get a closer look. As I moved I passed from the view of each central statue to the next, looming there in the center of the piazzo: one of them would always be watching me. I adopted a style of advancing ten steps, peeking up, back down below the edge and onward. It paid off in just a minute; as the wall brought me past an angle of the temple to where I could see the front entrance, I spotted the guards.

They weren't looking anywhere near my direction—they were facing each other and spitting as often as they talked. But I stared at the prospect of life in this desolate city until I lost track of time. I couldn't hear their voices, but they promised sound. They hardly moved but assured me that not everything here was as frozen as stone. And as much as they meant me ill, they reminded me of the size and temperature of the living. Stepping back a few paces, I eased over the wall and slipped to the temple's side. Closer to them, and a kind of danger I understood.

I listened from outside a wrecked stained glass window, and the last shreds of my theory, my desire, that this was a gang of kidnappers dissolved. Crackling wood echoing from several places, cries, the peculiar sound a lash makes, roars of laughter, the meaty sound of slaps and punches. I could smell the burning wood, the unwashed bodies, food, and more atop the background stench of rot. No doubt about it, there were scores of people in there, a population large enough that a whipped slave or a fist-fight did not gain everyone's attention. And filtering out to my ear from deep within, I caught the incoherent tones of two voices I had heard before. Barkarr's gravelly chuff, full of imperatives, and a whiny, broken counterpoint, full of denials. Farlo was there and he wasn't happy. And if Keilee was, I was betting she felt worse.

Altitude has always been my friend; it was time to climb. Compared to the modern counterpart, this Stargazer temple was practically bare, but I managed the tall side. Once I began to navigate the dome, the angle improved and my only concern was that it would not crack. There were rents in it large enough to swallow me, and I had no idea how well things could hold, so I avoided them. But the ancients had talents I had never seen. The sheer size of the dome was impressive, larger even than that set over the nave of the Hopeforgers. Carved into it at strategic spots were large glass windows, too high to have broken from vandalism or disorder. Most of the panes were thickly set with color, the kind you go to the Cups for. But I crawled to one circular portal near the top, set with dozens of smaller hexagonal panes in a lead grid-frame, and the outer rim was clear. I looked down upon the gang.

There were scores of beings arranged in camps at various spots around the formerly sacred space. Right in the center the dusty white marble statue facing me rose so that I was nearly looking him in the eye. Argens, I thought at first, as I noted the regal bearing and high crown, the eternal sun-flame in his outstretched hand. I saw the Stargazer badge at his chest as well, and far below me on the floor of the temple, his foot trod the head of a three-legged demon. But tucked at his waist was not the sword of the First of the First, but the flail of Cryss Altair, first Mark of the North. Before him on the cloth-draped altar stood the scale of judgement, mark of Ekhonon; his cloak was pinned with the Moment-Gem of Ma-Eldar, and a golden torc on his lowered arm had a serpent's head, sign of Khoirah. So this much was true—they practiced the apostasy of union in those days. Stories told the curse was brought down on Old Cryss because the nobility had courted the notion all the great heroes were really the same. I accepted that Argens was worshipped in various ways by the major sects. But this idea that he and Cryss, his rebellious vassal, and all these northern lords were one and the same, seemed to cross a line. Here was proof of their intent, carved in stone and thirty feet high.

But the present inhabitants of this place likely didn't trouble with questions of religion. I saw two clumps of bedrolls and small campfires to either side of the main entrance, each staffed by at least a dozen warlike figures engaged in eating, sparring, drinking and sleep.

Two or three smaller groupings dotted the side nave on my right; there was a kind of paddock near a far wall with cages, most empty but some rustling with indistinct movement. In the side-nave to my left, the degraded remnant of a Stargazer pleasure-compound was still recognizable. Once a beautifully crafted pavilion with split levels, couches, braziers and hanging plants, the area was now overgrown with creeping foliage; many of the benches had been pushed aside or wrecked, but not all. In some places, separated by space but still in plain view, there were a half-dozen women waiting by couches, and one was currently engaged serving desire from a large thug who had done whatever was needed to get past the ten fully armed guards at the edge. I noted, as she struggled beneath him, that her ankle was chained to the floor. The obvious lack of volition involved turned my stomach, and I knew I was looking on one of the few sights that could raise even a Stargazer's temper to the boiling point. I thought of Keilee, but though one of the other slaves was small she was not young enough.

I became consumed with the need to find out if she was here. There were places I could not see from this vantage, so I scanned the rest of the center area quickly before moving on. Several swarthy men stood armed by the altar, humans from the look of them, and a few steps from there Barkarr huddled with Farlo and a few others. Everything gave a sign of waiting—I saw the thin ex-prisoner start to speak, and his leader cuffed him to be quiet. I scrabbled to a new vantage point, this time tempting fate at a crack nearly over the center of the hall, just behind the statue's head. On the floor beneath the carved cape the wide thick flagstones were churned up, with a hole that looked familiar. Two more pock-faced guards stood sentinel there, and I knew there was trouble reeking from the whole arrangement. Back over the statue's shoulder towards the front of the temple I could see that in some of the cages by the wall the moving occupants were human. My instincts kicked, but that was only the answer to "where", not "why".

I knew I was going to need a distraction and ideas were coming to me. Desperate schemes, mostly, involving a big splash, temporary success and an enormous chance of failure. I grinned to think of them, and began to pick from the various ingredients the ones most fun. I wished that hole wasn't so close to where I'd have to land. But nothing is perfect.

The two hole-guards jumped away from the tunnel, and the show was on. One after the other, three of those enormous Bugs crawled up, wielding two spears apiece and wearing what appeared to be added plating. Following this trio was a low, heavy beetle-like thing with a snow white manikin on its back, smooth and oblong with too many sections and six legs. The featureless head slowly turned to both sides, and my flesh crawled. After that emerged a lithe, muscular elf with a longsword at his belt and a circlet of thin bronze on his head, his upper body wrapped in a sash of bright scarlet silk. He was short but clearly agile and quick, barefooted with a piercing look on his forward-thrusting head; the long nose and sharp chin made his face into a point. The entire population of the temple stopped and crowded forward towards the front of the altar as his procession came around to meet them. I noticed the gang, which must have numbered ten score persons or more, left plenty of room before the statue and altar as the thin crowned elf, clearly their leader, came up the steps to greet them. I scanned around and noted with some relief that the heavily armed guards by the female slave-couches evidently had orders, to remain at their posts. A name sussurated through the gathering group below and I caught it after a few seconds, "Salivaar... Salivaar..."

The Bugs halted to one side and the elves gave them a wide berth as well. The leader gestured gently with one arm for silence, which was immediately given.

"So," he intoned in a quiet scratchy voice, "Farlo here has returned to us." A ragged cheer started up, and died when the leader's gaze remained fixed on the fellow. "And we must wonder," he continued, "how."

Farlo stood there in terror, unable to make his jaw work. Barkarr and his loyal crew took a small step or two back until things became clearer.

"You escaped?" Salivaar asked, and Farlo slowly shook his head. Salivaar grinned and gestured to his flock, "The good man is a wizard, and never told us!" A few scattered laughs greeted this, and Farlo shook his head more vigorously. Salivaar leaned in with his hands slightly spread, "Well, then? I have only one more explanation, good fellow, and I don't think you'd like to hear me say it."

"I was freed!" Farlo squeaked, "a fellow posted surety for me. And I come straight here, 'cause that's the order Barkarr give us. Wasn't followed—"

"Yes," Salivaar cut in, "we are checking on that right now. But tell us, Farlo, who was this singular charitable citizen who came in the middle of the night to see you set at liberty. Do you know him? A friend of yours?"

It's rare to see a grown man actually squirm, with the shoulders and knees. Farlo bobbed his head in a meaningless way, trying to deny part of the suggested story, too terrified to correct the rest, ashamed to admit any of it. I could see reflections of his terror in the avid looks on all the firelit faces around.

"I don't, don't know his name, sir, only he come and signed a paper and let me go…" groans of derision drowned him out, but Salivaar seemed almost thoughtful.

"I must say," he mused, "I would have expected a spy to have a better story."

"Spy!" the cry went around the crowd, as if it were unexpected. "Kill him now!" some shouted, and others "Pox him!" or a few "Prove him out! The test!"

I was now throwing out any plan that involved escaping their attention; this crowd would never settle down before someone came back to report their guard was trussed. Bad for Farlo, but almost as bad for me—I needed to get down to those cages, check for Keilee, and get out. But it was looking increasingly as if only the center of the stage would be open to me. I wasn't as experienced as I would like for leading roles. I ran the checklist in my head as Salivaar settled his men down.

"Now then, fellows! You see why I must take the greatest care, for all of us, that our secret is not revealed. My patron has enemies, and the time is not yet ripe for us to seize the place we have been promised. Loath though I would be," he promised with a feral grin, "to lose one of my own, I cannot be too cautious. Barkarr—you were his overseer, what say you?"

I had finished my scan and seen not a single bow or crossbow—one mark to the good. On the other hand, every man-jack who could stand up was armed, and then there were the Bugs. I began to gauge distances as Barkarr managed to close his jaw and draw a shaky breath before his master.

"Pox him, sir."

Farlo cried out in terror as some in the crowd shouted their agreement. Playing to them, Salivaar slowly drew his longsword, which was incredibly rusty or perhaps made of old bronze. He showed it all around, then ran it lightly underneath his off-hand, drawing blood and letting it drip freely over the blade. He showed it to Farlo and cried out, "How then, Farlo? Are you willing to try and join the closest of my bodyguards?" The men nearest the altar cackled and exchanged slaps on the back with each other. I realized their faces and arms were not swarthy, and they were not mortal humans. They were elves, affected by some dread disease that Salivaar carried, survivors who had no better place—indeed no other place—than by their leader's side.

Farlo groveled on the stone floor and screamed his preference, until Barkarr savagely stomped on his throat. Even then, he guttered and choked "no" as the audience growled and cheered for it. Salivaar looked down on the lump of fear and made a decision. Slowly he resheathed his sword and held his arms up for silence. I saw that his hand was already no longer bleeding and my heart pounded out an extra few beats.

I tore my gaze away, knowing I had only minutes left to act. I could see the first leap clearly, and felt good about that. Not eight people in the city could make it, and two wouldn't try. Then I had options for getting down. I thumbed up a glass vial from my belt, and thought about where I could throw it to make the fire spread the fastest. Even with everything falling my way, the best chance would be that no one would expect me to run to the cages. I might have several seconds, no missiles, some confusion, a little fear, and could scan to see if she was there. Then I'd have to get out, and plan how to come back once Salivaar had gone.

He had them calmed down again. "My worthy followers," he called, "it is clear that Farlo here does not wish to take that test."

Groans and shouts fired from the crowd to the man on the floor. "And I will not force it upon him—I want only the willing, as well as the strong, among my closest crew, and it seems clear that Farlo is neither." Some laughter at this, and Farlo, nothing bothered by verbal abuse, came up to his knees with a watery smile on his face, nodding his gratitude.

"Besides," Salivaar said grandly, "I have another test we can use."

The room hushed as if it were suddenly empty. An incoherent cry of horror emanated from the kneeling man, as Salivaar the slender king of Old Cryss smiled and gestured one of his bodyguards toward a cabinet set behind the altar. I looked at Farlo and saw the stone beneath his knees was puddled; he would have fallen backwards to crawl away if Barkarr and the others had not kicked him upright. He babbled his innocence, his preference, his deference, in half-words and shattered phrases, while the guard brought around a cloth-covered plate. The temple buzzed with anticipation. I felt I was watching a gladiatorial contest; despite no weapons, there was death in the air.

A series of alto clicks cut through the noise, from where the Insectirs hunched waiting. Many of the warriors standing around jumped and all conversation ceased. Salivaar produced a small wooden box from his waist, and turned the crank on its side emitting a series of long and short clicks. The Bugs responded in kind, and Salivaar said "I have nearly forgotten our esteemed allies in all this, who have just reminded me that our next installment is due. Bring one over now and then we will continue to prove our good man's loyalty here."

A ruffian close to the cage wall produced a large key and opened one cell apparently at random. Reaching in he pulled out first a thin arm and then the rest of an urchin-sized prisoner and dragged her towards the altar area. She kicked at him and shouted how her father and his friends were coming, and they would all be in *big trouble* then, which produced chuckles from the parting ranks. As she came closer I saw her and it was good news and bad news at the same time. I didn't have to look for Keilee anymore. New plan, trying to snatch her from the center of the group, more fun. But it beat following the Bugs and asking permission.

"You rat, you carker!" Keilee shrieked, still more angry than scared even with the man-high insects in plain view. Salivaar flicked a glance at her and then gestured with his head to the waiting monsters. Her captor flung her bodily by the elbow and she fell hard in a heap on the stone before the low beetle-thing. Keilee bounced up holding her arm and backed away a few steps. She froze in place and I figured it was finally sinking in that she was meat. But she stooped down, snatched up a broken corner of flagging, whirled and fired it directly at Salivaar's head. He flinched to one side with speed that caught my eye and barked a laugh.

"You carker!" she screamed with the freedom children rarely get to curse without their parents nearby. "I'll get... you won't... you..." her speech slowed as if she was having trouble making her tongue work. I knew that had never been a problem for her before; I realized with a chill that none of the Bugs had moved, especially not the albino. No features on its face and not a quiver from any of its limbs, but it was facing Keilee directly as if it could see her. Without sense or explanation, the girl just lay down on the flagging and fell deeply asleep. Only then did the glistening thing move, stepping off its mount, picking up the prize and placing it on the beetle in its stead.

I was down to seconds remaining, and the game kept changing. I put away the vial and picked out another crystal gem, trying to gauge the spot below where it would have the most effect. Something was still missing from my hasty plan—surprise would not be enough, I needed fear. But it was getting too late even for desperate plans. Feldspar rejoiced at the low odds and heaping risk, because he didn't mind if tonight was his last to live. But another part of me, the one named Simith, wanted to win.

Salivaar took one step down closer to Farlo and asked him in a paternal tone.

"Now then, Farlo, you claim you are loyal to me, yes?" Farlo nodded helplessly. "And if so, then you are worthy, are you not? Worthy to remain in this band." Now the victim did not nod, or seem to breathe or even move. "Come then, and take the test, of loyalty and worth." The diseased guard with the plate stepped forward and Salivaar slipped off the cloth, unveiling a magnificent crown set with seven gems.

He raised it high and shouted "Behold! The infallible artifact provided by my patrons, which always confirms the guiltless and punishes the traitor. Farlo now, of his own free will, comes forward to take the test of his worth." The thin thug, whose blubbering flinched at the sound of his name, seemed minded at first to continue refusing the honor being offered. But he quieted down, slowly stood and began to advance towards the altar. I thought he moved like a sleep-walker, and snapped my eyes back to the white Insectir; it was standing stock-still with one hand on Keilee's back and its blind oval face in Farlo's direction.

In my head I heard Kama's voice reading the description I had shown him only last evening.

Oh wondrous Brow! What sword can match your keen beauty? What palace rise above your braided bands? Can the allure of any human form approach the grace, the breathtaking sweep of gold and gem that in you are by nature mingled?

Farlo stumbled on the first altar-step, almost fell but recovered and clumped to the top with leaden legs. Salivaar held the crown overhead so that its gems caught the torchlight. I could feel the corners of my mouth pulling back beneath the mask into a grimace of anticipation, but in my mind Kama kept reading.

At each of the perfect seven heights above the triune bands, a gem set as if grown from seed... and in the front center, resting upon the very brow itself, there lies the finest work of the Dwarven lords, for which the treasures of dragons are themselves easily forfeit. The violet star blazes out in watchful might, an unstoppable ward against the forces of Despair. The Browstone sleeps not in protection of its rightful wearer, and as tirelessly destroys the impure who dare to sully the circlet with their unclean heads.

Salivaar brought the crown down slowly to Farlo's skull, and his hands were still on the metal when I saw the smoke. The room broke into eager jeers as the hair smoldered and his flesh turned black. His face burst into flame, prompting a cheer and some coins exchanged in the back rows. To the side I saw the blind albino Bug turn away and draw out some straps to tie down the sleeping body before him. Farlo, returned to himself, started to scream and claw at the crown until his hands ignited. He fell to his knees already a mass of flame; his last three or four groans of agony were automatic, the consequence of his still being able to breathe. But that stopped, and the charred husk of him fell to the steps with a hollow-sounding impact, scattering a basket-worth of fine ash up into the drafts. The crown was unscathed, and the only way to tell which end of him had been the head.

A fire grew inside me too, and I realized it was anger. Normally that would mean the job was off. But tonight, after seeing all I had, I knew I was in Astor's arms—danger-drunk, as the legends of him said. I knew what it meant now. As soon as the Brow came in sight, Feldspar had assumed the snatch-and-grab was on. I let him think it, while I quickly formulated a third plan. Same leap, keep the gem, but now I needed a speech.

And fortunately I had one, that I never got to use, ready for delivery.

I gathered myself and dove arms-first into the crevice, my right hand gently letting the gem go to fall in front of the statue down to the altar. I reached across the open space with every muscle, caught the statue at the collar of his cape. When the gem hit the altar and shattered, its flash was visible even to me on the other side. The shout of surprise and pain was almost simultaneous. I drew breath and pitched my voice to carry.

Blasphemers! You dare to profane this place, my home, with your sordid habits and vile talk. Begone before I strike you down for your sins!

Men began calling out, falling down, even screaming. I kipped over the statue's shoulder, sprang out to seize his outstretched arm, swung and released, arcing down to land directly on the altar itself. I slipped a bit on the cloth runner and grabbed up the scales for balance. The crowd was boiling like a hill of ants, and the giant ant-things were even worse. Except for the blind albino, whose head faced directly at me but otherwise didn't move. Salivaar, his face a foot from my knee, was looking my way but seeing nothing. I was very glad to cuff the side of his head with the scales and he flopped to the altar step. Justice served. I knew I had only seconds to act, before the vision of two hundred enemies cleared. To one side was the crown, to the other Keilee. I was getting ready to lie to Feldspar about why we were here, when I decided to stay still for a bit.

Some of the villains actually had fled the building, and many more were crying out that everyone should. But most of them tripped or ran into each other as they fell back; soon when they could see again there wouldn't be much for them to fear. I saw a clear path to Keilee and figured I could bowl over that shiny abomination without much trouble. Once again, I decided to stay still for a bit, and that struck me as troubling.

Barkarr had staggered closer to the front by accident, and I could see his pupils widening a tad as he struggled to focus. I froze in place atop the altar, and he squinted my way.

"Did—did Argens send you?" his tone was so respectful his voice cracked. I tried to make my laugh sound holy and righteous. Still, I wanted Barkarr to join his boss on the steps. As I reached behind me for my weapon I froze, and my heart dropped into my groin. There was no explaining a coincidence like that. If I fought Barkarr with the *noun-chakas*, Jonn Simith was gone. Feldspar was indifferent to that consequence, but I was stubborn. More than ever it was time to go—and this time, when I didn't move, I realized it wasn't my choice.

The white Bug was standing stock-still, and I felt in addition to my usual skin-crawling revulsion a sense of horror *inside* me. Barkarr stood just out of sword-reach, his vision cleared but still puzzled and unsure; he glanced down at his unconscious leader and drew his sword. At that precise moment, the hubbub at the main door grew, as thugs still trying to get out were being pushed aside by one of their number coming in. "Boss!" he shouted over the din, "Boss, Preeto's knocked out! Somebody's on this side!"

I needed to move my feet. Now. There was a whisper in my head, that I should probably just go to sleep, but I was a man used to winning such arguments. I reached down and yanked up the runner cloth covering the altar, spinning it around my head, then whipping it suddenly out to the side. Perfect—it wrapped around the white Bug's ankles and caught. I yanked hard, it toppled to the ground so that its blind head bounced, and a string snapped inside me. I was free to go. Barkarr's face was closing down into hatred now, and men were turning back to face the commotion at the altar.

No one in the temple was more surprised than Feldspar when I feinted at the crown, and then vaulted off to the side, directly at the Insectirs. The warriors were still dazed by the bright flash, and their leader was on his back, doing the same thing most bugs do in that position, only much larger and more unnerving. I kicked him out of my way, avoided the snap of the beetle's side-ways jaws, and reached in to snag Keilee up in my arms. Feldspar was only starting to register his outrage when I doubled down, and darted the wrong way, further back into the temple and away from the main entrance. In five steps I was behind the statue out of sight from most of the thugs; in two more I had thrown myself directly into the hole. By the time Barkarr or anyone else got there, it would be as if I had disappeared.

I half-tumbled, half-scrambled deeper into the nightmare hole, gagging with the need to not be there and trying to hold my breath. It was tall enough to stand, not shored or walled but tunneled in a way that looked uneven yet glossy. The musk here was stronger than that of any animal in the Overlord's public menagerie, and the reek of sewage mingled with it. I was convinced the air was poisonous. But what awaited me back in the temple was hardly conducive to long life either. I stumbled on into complete darkness.

I could only use one hand to trail on the wall, but was sure I passed a half-dozen openings; I took the third one to my left before I stopped. There was no sound at all from behind me, no drips or clunks ahead. I figured the temple for an uproar, but I must have come further than it seemed. Always, in the background was the distant suggestion of something scrambling over the hard earth floor. Underfoot I felt the tunnel starting to angle downward, and I was already further below ground than I liked.

At that moment, Feldspar rather tersely suggested this would be a good place to leave the kid and go back for the Brow. Sneaky bastard, I actually put her down and half-turned. In three steps, she could have been lost forever unless I risked a light. I turned back, knelt beside her to feel her pulse and breath, and finally let Feldspar fully in on the news. The girl was the mission, this time around. Then he hit me with everything he had.

The demon-blasted hells she is. The Brow is the mission; pay, risk, the service of Hope, everything right there. The brat kid, that was just for Simith. And Simith doesn't exist—I flinched as I thought it, but I also grinned a little.

Yeah, Simith exists; too late now. He knows people, they like him. And so what, yes, he likes them too! Walking in the daytime without a false nose is refreshing once in a while; maybe those who only wear masks should try it.

Our commission is to W'starrah Altieri. You want her to be disappointed in you, never see you again? It was a weak attempt, and I was ready.

We've completed the commission. We know where the Brow is, and we shall write to tell her as soon as we escape these Bug-infested tunnels.

That stopped him for a second, and I gathered Keilee in again to continue, seeking a way up this time.

Twenty thousand silver pieces!

Hah, do you think the Lavender Lady, when we tell her where the Brow is, will come down here to get it herself? Never fear, that money will still be offered us.

The greatest stealthic in the city stomped off toward the back of my mind to sulk, and I tried to orient myself without a light. The air was closing in, not getting better, and I was pretty sure I couldn't stay underground too long. I needed up. And for that, I needed light.

The lantern played around the intersection I had returned to, and I saw other holes and tunnels peppering the walls too small for any Bug. I could reach my arm into them, though I felt not the slightest inclination to do so. Sure enough, one large tunnel came in from above at an odd angle I might never have found by feeling around. I wondered if Feldspar might lend his skill to getting up there with Keilee in tow. He wondered if perhaps I tugged hard enough, I might be able to cark myself. But when I backed up for a running start, he came along by the next to last step and we just made it.

Keilee, far from awakening, started to snore, and I became a little concerned. What had that abomination done to her, and would she be alright? The air couldn't be much better for her than it was for me—I was starting to cough and eye-stars obscured what little I could discern by lantern. The tunnel leveled off after only a few steps, and I moved on for several anxious minutes choosing whichever turning seemed likely to lead higher. This was a gigantic maze, which suggested more Bugs than I was comfortable thinking about. My mind began to wander even as my breathing became more ragged and loud. I saw Farlo igniting, Salivaar going down under my blow, then the statue behind me starting to talk and move in angry wrath. The walking-waking dreams wouldn't stop and I was taking any turn as soon as it showed up. Suddenly I realized the scrambling sound was no longer distant. I swung the lantern's eye in towards my leg, but some kind of phosphorescence in the stone picked up a residual glow and I found I could dimly see the Bug coming down the tunnel towards me.

I had no bearings at all—still breathing loud and with no idea how far it was back to the last turning. I shrank against one wall as the monster, shaped very much like an ant except it was longer than a guard dog, almost filled the tunnel. It drew closer to me with a steady pace, and I saw behind the enormous mandibles were four sections and eight legs, but laid out like an ant in most every way. I thought it was thicker or had a ridgeback at first, but then I saw that there was something long and bundled strapped to its back. I eased out the *noun-chakas* and prepared to strike, every nerve keyed for a fight to the end. It came on without pause and my spine started to shout in favor of running away.

Don't move, came the thought, still sulking. *Can't see you. Fool.*

It would be just like him to get me killed in order to vent his spite. But I held my breath and squeezed against the wall. The thing lumbered on by, antennae twitching with reports but apparently orders were orders. I thought again about the slick, white leader Bug and its awful powers. How many were there? How many could it control? This one was already twenty steps past me and Feldspar was chuckling about the cowards he had to put up with. Fine, let him feel superior, I might need him to show off later.

I burst out coughing hard enough to bring up solids, and started to jog with every breath coming torn and choppy. The next intersection seemed to waft in something a little fresher, and my heart rose—until I saw the line of Bugs crawling across my path. These were light grey and about as big as housecats, scores of them in single file clearly illumined by the glowstones poking from the walls. As with the giant ant-thing, these ignored me while they plodded past, and I had time to wonder how many of them there were, unsuspected here in the heart of the city. Well, not in the heart, that was the point—but I knew where some of these tunnels came out. Salivaar had spoken of these Bugs as "allies" and someone else as a "patron". Those were not happy thoughts. I couldn't even be certain why the Bugs needed humans, though I had some likely guesses. Still, if Keilee was going to be food, with the number of Bugs I'd already seen—the city would be empty in a month.

The line ended at last and I charged across into a side tunnel that seemed narrow but—praise Astor—also led up. The end was covered with boards and bracken which I pushed aside, and then I was out into an empty avenue in the lee of an enormous domed building. Old Cryss was quiet and still, but the sewage-laced air tasted like it had sugar in it and I just sagged against the wall and filled my lungs with life as my head cleared.

With the moons to orient I made my way easily back to the river. No need for a secret tunnel now; I came in a bit below the ruined bridge but got to the pilings. With Keilee over my back I hopped more easily—the sun would be up within the hour and already there were some stirrings on the opposite shore. The only thing more annoying than a sea gull in your way is one that's been sleeping. But I picked and chose the spots, kicking a choice few into the water where they squawked and flapped and made their way to another roost with their dignity in tatters.

On the near shore I had a thought. Finding a secure place under The Boards to tuck my drowsy bundle, I slipped away to the alley behind my house. When Keilee began to stir in the morning light, I had my drab brown and green outfit back on and was gently shaking her arm.

"Well, ahm, well, there you are!" I exclaimed with an affected yawn. She shook her head and sat up, her eyes not able to credit where she was or who she was with. I could see she remembered everything up until she fell asleep. I prompted her because the way she told this tale would have a big influence on mine.

"Where have you been little one? Your family has been looking for days, I just thought I'd step out early and see—and here, ahm, here you are, why—"

"I was kidnapped!" she insisted to me, and I let my thin eyebrows rise in astonishment. "These mean men took me right from the alley, and put me in a bag and then I was in a cage in some stinky old temple. I think I was in the old city! And there was a *huge* statue of somebody, and the food was awful, and there were these enormous bugs too, and a man with a rat-face who tried to give me to them…"

115

I nodded seriously and relaxed inside as she rattled on. No one would pay a silver bit for this tale, and poor Keilee would certainly be punished. The more accurate her descriptions the less likely she would be believed. I thought about the way I could word my letter to W'starrah Altieri, as Keilee kept talking and the ships down-dock started loading for the day's sailing. Something cryptic, perhaps, and with enough details to convince her of my witness to it. I might have as much trouble being believed as Keilee, if it came to that. But no matter—she could test me for truth if she really doubted, the first five thousand was as good as mine. And I felt sure she would want the Brow liberated from its present place, so more work beckoned. Perhaps I could deliver the letter through Ekatarinye; it would be nice to make sure she was alright.

Keilee had finally wound down her tale and I let my brow contract a bit as I asked a few questions to help warn her. "But then, mistress, how came you here to this side? Did you escape?" She said nothing and shrugged, looking down. "Why would they let you go?" She looked back up and I could see that she was considering her options—perhaps a lie, and quicker punishment would be best. I patted her shoulder reassuringly. "Well, I am delighted that you are well after all this time. Three days, my goodness—and terrible food or none as you said, you must be starving. Oh and you are quite dirty, madam I must say."

I brushed her off a bit as she stood up, and her review of her pockets turned up a piece of stone. A bit of the temple floor flagging had gotten lodged there, maybe a remnant of what she had so bravely flung at Salivaar. I looked at it warily as she held it out.

"What is this?" she asked. I took it from her and put on my best scholarly air.

"Well, it's a kind of granite in fact."

"Is it valuable? Like a gem?"

"Well no, ahm, in fact, you're making a common mistake, mistress." I thought if I showed off a little I could calm her agitation and get her away from where this rock was last seen. "A stone, in most cases, is like a gem, or truly has gem-materials inside it. This granite here, is not really one thing but has several ingredients in it—some sand, really, and ahm, those dark bits there are likely some sort of mica, and then there's feldspar—"

"Feldspar!" she exclaimed, and I cursed him for tricking me into talking. Tired of Simith, he wanted the secret out, the bastard. But Keilee was thinking only of wealth. "That's a gem, isn't it? Where is it?"

I pointed to the tiny white-red-brown bits between the strata. "All of that, most likely, is feldspar."

"But that—those bits—those are stuck into all kinds of rocks, good and bad ones."

"Yes," I smiled, "it's very common indeed, and usually not too bright or easy to spot. You might say we never, ahm, really see feldspar, even when it's right in front of us. So we get a bit lazy and say 'this is granite' as if it were a new thing when really it is a mixture."

She took back the stone and looked it over. "Like people," she said suddenly. "So if everything is really all mixed together—how do we tell the good from the bad?" I looked into her eyes and followed her quicksilver thought—the men who had taken her, an instant before they grabbed and stuffed her in a sack, looked like every other nameless adult. It had become tough for me to swallow—and still, even now I could not lie to her. She was brave, and we had shared risk—Astor forbade it.

"Well, that is indeed a difficult question. With stones, we can test them before we start to build, and the bad ones will crack. With people too, ahm, we must, well, pay close attention. And stick together. The mica and the sand, by themselves, do not make strong buildings. The separation, that's what hurts us…" I could hardly understand where I was going with my speech—I was starting to sound like the healer. But as we turned and climbed the steps to The Boards in the dawn, I looked out to the old city across the Tepid. I thought about men who were separate, and bad. I heard Talishaya's voice calling and saw the family out already on search. I waved to them and the lovely girl put her hands to her face and shrieked with relief.

As they ran toward us, Keilee looked up and said "So we should stick together I guess. To stay strong." I nodded and tried to maintain my banal, meaningless face of weak good will.

A moment later, I was one bit mixed into a large block of people, all kinds and colors, giving Jonn Simith far too much credit for finding the child, and the infamous Feldspar none at all. With that I was content. That, and the prospect of five and twenty thousand pieces of silver. Perhaps, I suggested to myself, real life would be worth living after all.

If you liked this story, please leave a review somewhere. To learn more about William L. Hahn, sign up for the Gentle Reminders on his website.

GLOSSARY

Altair Way	street	main thoroughfare of Cryssigens
Ancient	language	tongue of the heroes, dragons and beings of power; mortals may not lie when using it
Areghel	hero	first king of the Percentalion, hero of martial wizards
Argens	city	capital city of the Southern Empire, on the central western coast, named for its hero
Argens Demonbender		hero-aspect, major form of devotion to Argens, currently outlawed, emphasizing sorcerous lore and mastery of demons
Argens Hopeforger		hero-aspect, major form of devotion to Argens, emphasizing courage, light and leadership
Argens Stargazer		hero-aspect, major form of devotion to Argens, emphasizing foresight and love
Argensian Empire		aka the Southlands, vast Elven Empire established by Argens, capital city also named Argens
Astor	hero	Perilsgroom, hero of Stealthics from ancient days
Bald Top	mountain	small loaf-shaped mountain the border hills
Battle of Broken Chains		Dolphin 2001 ADR, first victory of the rebellion over Loyalist forces of the North Mark
Battle of the Razor		pivotal battle of ancient times, Despair was ejected from the Lands forever in the year 0 ADR
Battle of Tor Perite		site of decisive battle (Serpent, 2001 ADR) that defeated Viridian XXVII and put Yula I on the throne of Argens
Bedou-uu	race	desert dwelling nomads of the Shimmering Mindsea
bought badge	phrase	insulting term for an officer who purchased a commission he could not earn
Brow of the Ecclesiast		artefact, mystic crown with fabulous powers, burns the unworthy wearer

centar		unit of soldiers, ten dekents = 100 men
Cesmir	barony	southern barony of the North Mark
cestus	weapon	spiked metal glove used by gladiators
Charnel Testing		an attempt to wear the Brow of the Ecclesiast, which results in death by burning for the unworthy
Conar	city	capital of the kingdom of Men, named for its hero
Cryssians	sect	devotees of Cryss Altair
Cryssigens	city	capital city of the North Mark, wealthy and Color-ful
Dagnaluviran	song	heroic tale of love between Dagnar and Elosira
dekent		unit of soldiers, one dekent equals ten men (led by a dekentar)
dekentar		junior officer's rank in the army or guards
Devouting Sinter		monastery of holy men in Gaden, bordering the Shimmering Mindsea
Earthcut River		runs through Gaden and Cesmir to the Western Sea
Ekhonon	hero	second son of Conar, judgement and architecture
Exemplars	hero	minor heroes of ancient times
Far Mark		recently recolonized duchy of the Argensian Empire, next to the Swords of Stone
Fire Grip	title	City Commander of Cryssigens, regent of the Mark in the absence of the Overlord
Flame of the First		mild oath, reference to Argens who caught a slice of the Sun in his hand
Gaden	barony	east-central barony of the North Mark
Gelvorging Deep		thick forested area, unsettled and hiding bandits or monsters
glassteel		clear substance harder than metal
Grog's Lees	tavern	modest, in The Boards neighborhood of Cryssigens
Highforge	title	rank given to the Preacher worthy of the Brow of the Ecclesiast
Horn of the Serpent		relic of those devoted to Khoirah the Betrayer, stolen by Trekelny and now lost (*see Three Minutes to Midnight*)

House Cups	title	heads of various Colors in Cryssigens, wielding great wealth and influence
Ides of the Dolphin		date, mid-point of the 2nd month, 15th
Imperial Domain		barony, gorgeous settled lands adjacent to Argens and direct vassalage to the Emperor
Insectir	monster	giant bug creatures, repugnant to Elves
intakta volar	language	in Ancient: I wish for healing
kemetaria	feature	burial ground, a Despairing practice to put bodies under the earth instead of cremation
Khoirah	anti-hero	the Betrayer, third son of Conar who treated with Despair in ancient times
lith	drug	performance enhancing, addictive, poisonous
Ma-Eldar	hero	Hopelord of Elves, father of Argens
Master of Horse		leader of all Imperial cavalry
North Mark		northern duchy of Argens, with a history of rebellion; capital city Cryssigens
noun-chakas	weapon	two wooden hafts connected by a few links of chain
Nubian	race	tall black Men living in the Southern jungle, fearsome warriors
odd as three feet		phrase, reference to demonic creatures, meaning something is very strange or unexpected
Old City		northeastern quarter of Cryssigens, once wealthy but long since abandoned
Overlord	title	aka North Mark, title of the ruler of that duchy
Palace of the Sun		castle, Emperor's dwelling in Argens' capital
Patriarch	title	church leader in a nation or great city
pentadek		unit of soldiers, five dekents = 50 men
piazzo		center of abandoned Old Cryss, open paved area with temples and more
Ring of Peace	miracle	Telholian invocation creating a no-magic, no-violence zone
Salva Way		bordering the piazzo in Old Cryss
Scapegrace Street		bordering the piazzo in Old Cryss

Shard Demon	monster	held prisoner beneath the palace in Cryssigens
Shimmering Mindsea		large sandy desert between Argens and the Swords of Stone
silversteel		magical metal, unbreakable and rare
somnos	drug	induces sleep
Son of the Sun	title	honorific title for the Emperor, successor to Argens
strategos	title	senior officer's rank in the army or guard
Sun Throne		Emperor's throne in Argens, also a reference to the Emperor's rank
Tamar	city	small trading city about a day's journey from Cryssigens
Telhol	hero	fourth son of Conar, hero of peace and healing
Tepid River		separates Cryssigens from the Old City on its way to the Western Sea
The Boards		poor neighborhood in Cryssigens bordering the River Cryss
Tralmachia	barony	northernmost barony of the North Mark, mountainous and isolated
Viper	sect	secret police under Viridian, now outlawed

SHARDS OF LIGHT I: THE RING AND THE FLAG

A Sword and Sorcery novel from the Lands of Hope.

Newly-graduated imperial officer Justin is convinced he has no future, and hearing the details of the secret mission he's assigned for the Emperor won't change his mind. Civil War threatens the North Mark. Justin must race against time to form a company, and lead his men into the center of the web; but what happens when his loyalty to the Empire means the death of those who follow him?

available as eBook and in print
ISBN 978-3-95681-094-7

SHARDS OF LIGHT III: PERILOUS EMBRACES

A Sword and Sorcery novel from the Lands of Hope.

As the city of Cryssigens spirals towards chaos, its leaders scheme in secret to alter the future. But W'starrah Altieri, priestess of Argens Stargazer, already sees it. Can she balance her loyalty to the North Mark against the threat of an imperial invasion, and locate the mystic artefact whose touch will either unite the land in peace or end her life in fire? And what chance, in all this tumult, for the most beautiful woman in the kingdom to find the love of her life before Argens requires her death?

Coming soon

SHARDS OF LIGHT IV: SHARDS OF LIGHT

A Sword and Sorcery novel from the Lands of Hope.

The North Mark teeters toward a rebellion that will bring crushing retribution from the Argensian Empire. Only three heroes, barely acquainted and scattered far, have the chance between them to avert war and ruin. Can Captain Justin escape the death-trap of Tralmachia and return in time for the crucial vote? Does Feldspar have the skill and courage to revisit the Old City and snare the fabled Brow of the Ecclesiast from its current home among bandits and Bugs? Will W'starrah Altieri, beautiful priestess who hired the stealthic and loves the soldier, see into the conspiracy's heart before the wave of fire she has foreseen engulfs her and the city of Cryssigens? The fate of a kingdom is reflected in these mortal Shards of Light.

Coming soon

Two millenia of peace are coming to an end.

For twenty centuries the Lands of Hope prospered from their Heroes' peace, but suffer now from their absence. Chaos grows in the central kingdom of the Lands of Hope known as the Percentalion. Even the bravest adventurers seem unable to travel in or out safely. The sundered populations are trapped there, beyond communication and without hope.

Worse yet, the liche Wolga Vrule plots escape from his extra-worldly prison to unleash a tide of undeath, and enlists the Earth Demon Kog, who ruled the Percentalion millennia ago, as an uneasy ally.

On the western coast of the Lands of Hope, Solemn Judgement comes ashore, having journeyed with his father across the ocean. Solemn arrives both a stranger and and orphan, driven to complete the lore his father died to give him. Will he discover Wolga Vrule's plan in time to prevent the return of Despair?

continues in "Eye of Kog"

THE PLANE OF DREAMS

A standalone novel from the Lands of Hope

In the southern empire of Argens just roiled by the rebellion of Yula, a band of adventurers returns from the Shimmering Mindsea bearing enormous treasure and minus one of its members. The Tributarians, unaware of the growing threat to the waking world, embark on separate plans. But the spirit of the hero lives on in all of them, as their good deeds have consequences beyond their original intention. Will it be enough to avert the peril they have unwittingly brought about?

This first epic-length tale set in the Lands of Hope features a complex world and intelligent, dedicated characters whose actions entwine over distances and beyond their own comprehension. Like any world worth living in, the Lands have humor, mystery, horror and action to delight and entertain the reader.

available as eBook and in print
ISBN 978-3-95681-066-4